SUNSET BLOOD

WADE PETERSON

DAVID W. WRIGHT

STERLING & STONE

SUNSET BLOOD

Chapter One

A BREEZE CAME FROM THE WEST, POWERFUL ENOUGH TO SET the old farm's broken windmill squeaking, but unable to clear the afternoon heat inside the barn or soothe the rising tempers of the outlaws who lived there.

Cal Jones lounged on a pile of flour sacks covering an old saddle bench, resting his head against the wall where an open knothole sent the breeze shooting down his collar for some small relief. He held a small wooden cross in his hand, the grain worn smooth over the past year under his handling and kept dry by a swatch of calico. The heat was enough to set a man's brains boiling, and the memento was the only thing that cooled it down as of late.

Four of the notorious Wild Six lay about the barn — Pete Carter, Silas Beasley, Ben Horn, plus himself — on account of the farmhouse's collapsed roof and rotten floorboards likely covering a nest of rattlers as not. They laid about on rickety stools, moldering mattresses, and wobbly chairs scavenged from the farmhouse, setting them just so to avoid the afternoon sunlight lancing through the holes in the roof and walls.

"I bet he's drinking it all," Pete said. He scratched at his dark beard, making Cal wonder if he'd finally grown it long enough to attract fleas.

"Takes a while," Silas said, adjusting his hat as a sunbeam from a recent hole in the roof ambushed him. His beanpole frame leaned back, chair creaking on two legs as he set his boot heels on a barrel of nails. He gave his fair hair and scalp a vigorous scratching before setting his hat low over his eyes.

Pete twisted in his chair and squinted across the yard. "Doesn't take this long." He cut a tobacco plug and set it in his lower lip, deepening his perpetual scowl.

"You're welcome to go help," Silas said. "Don't know how yellin' is gonna make water seep out the ground faster, but I expect a smart fella like you figured that out already." He gave a lopsided grin and tapped a finger aside a nose crooked from an old break. It was a gesture that worked miracles for Silas with the ladies, but also one he'd learned got under Pete's skin.

"Maybe he found a copperhead and got bit," Ben said, the small man wiping dust from his spectacles before hooking them back over his ears.

"That'd explain it," Silas said.

Pete spat a stream of tobacco juice into the dirt floor. "He'd have yelled if he did. Snake bite takes a while to kill you."

"If you say so," Silas said.

"I do. Saw a guy nailed by a cottonmouth once, took him a whole day to die."

"I thought we were talking about copperheads," Silas said.

Pete whipped a pebble over Silas's head, which clattered in the far corner. "Same thing, more or less."

Silas tipped up his hat for a glance at Pete, then settled it back with a smirk.

"He should be back by now," Pete muttered.

The cross spun around Cal's fingers. Hell of a thing for a man like him to carry. Might make people think he was a religious man, which was why it usually stayed wrapped in the calico and tucked away in his pocket. Today something made him take it out, spin it 'round his fingers, think about the way it used to rest against her skin.

A rock skittered outside, followed by footsteps and clanking. Rubin Bauer turned the corner, holding the water barrel in a bear-hug, waddling it over to its usual place in a darkened corner. He shook out a bandanna and wiped the sweat from his face, then combed his thinning hair back in place with blunt fingers.

"Took you long enough," Pete said.

Rubin tugged at his sweat-darkened shirt and adjusted his braces back over his shoulders. "Had to water the horses, didn't I? Saved yours for last."

Pete held up a middle finger. Silas chuckled.

"Bryan better come back with a bottle," Silas said. "Now that we got water, we just need some whiskey to go with it."

"My brother has the list," Pete said.

"And the last of the haul from the Marlowe job," Ben said. "If he don't come back with it, we gotta start looking for other another way. Maybe sneak into Sunset and break a few windows."

"Or find another train to hit," Pete said and turned to Cal. "Right, Trigger?"

Cal flipped the cross front-to-back, side-to-side. "The nice thing about trains is there's always one comin'," he said without looking up.

"I'd rather he come back with bacon. Or a sack of flour, not full of *veevils*," Rubin said.

"*Wee*-vills," Pete corrected.

"*Whee*-vills," Rubin repeated. "As I said."

"No, you been out in the sun so long it's baking the English off your dirty German tongue. Damn gutter talk is what that is."

Rubin's face clouded, and he rested his hand near his belt knife. "Not gutter talk."

"Quit hackin' on him, Pete," Silas said. "Some of us are trying to sleep."

"I don't recall askin' you, Silas," Pete said. "And you wouldn't sleep so easy if it was your horse he was treating poorly."

"Somebody's got to be watered last," Silas said.

"That may be," Pete said, "but it better be somebody else's animal next time."

The problem with Pete, Cal thought, was his brain was constantly simmerin' with thoughts about the wrongs the world inflicted on Pete and Pete alone. The day's heat likely brought it to boil, turning him into a steam-powered jackass. Cal folded the calico over the cross and put it in his pocket, pressing it briefly to make sure it wouldn't slip out. If Pete were about to explode, best it be aimed at him than the others. Cal was pretty sure he could keep himself from killing the asshole.

"What you gonna dream about, Silas?" Cal asked.

Silas smiled. "Walkin' into Sunset, flush, no lawman in sight, discovering there's a new sporting girl at the saloon with a honey voice that won't make me feel bad at all for walking out the next morning broke as hell."

Pete sniffed. "Be better off walking into the general store and so we don't have to pay Buzby's for supplies. They even got flour without no *wee*-vils."

"If you're gonna dream like that, Pete, you may as well make it San Francisco," Cal said.

"I hear there's always a cool breeze," Ben said.

Cal smiled. "More than that. The ladies there all wear those Frenchie dresses, each one so pretty your head'll just twist right off from all the looking."

"What about the whiskey?" Silas asked.

"They stuff they sell in Sunset may as well be vinegar by comparison," Cal said.

"Must be expensive, San Francisco," Rubin said.

"People drop silver dollars on the street and not even bother picking them up. An enterprising man could make a fortune with nothing more than a broom and dustpan."

"Bullshit," Pete said. "If it were like that, everyone'd be there."

"Guess you won't know until you go out and see for yourself, Pete."

"Have you seen it, Trigger?" Rubin asked.

Cal shrugged. "Fixin' to. Heard some stories of those heading that way, just haven't gotten around to it yet." The cross dug into his hip, and he shifted. "Might be a fine place to move on, come to think of it. We could do well there."

It might even be a little true, Cal thought. It was only a matter of time until the territory got statehood and Sunset's sheriff got delusions of higher office. Jed Scott didn't have time to go after the Six now, but he'd make the time if he thought it'd make his name sing in the governor's ears.

Pete sent another stream of brown spit into the dirt. "That's a dumbass idea, Trigger. What the hell do we know about San Francisco? Where'd we get a hideout, huh? What kind of crows they got there, and how tough are they? We'd as likely wind up starving or dead before we figured out a score."

"You're right, Pete. How could I leave all this?" Cal spread his hands to take in the barn.

Silas laughed.

Pete rose from his rickety chair. "The problem with you, Trigger, is you only know how to rob trains."

"I reckon they got trains in San Francisco," Cal said.

"We need to think bigger, Cal. There's banks."

"We tried a bank once, Pete. It didn't suit."

"That was an accident," Pete said.

"And now we can't go into Sunset anymore."

"Says you. I'm not sure what's got you spooked."

Jed stood and stepped to Pete, forcing the man to look up. "That's right, Pete. Says me. You got a problem?"

The rest of the barn stilled. Rubin looked to Ben, who waved him down. Silas tipped his hat up and peeked out.

Pete met his eye, and Cal could see him wanting to take a swing. Cal shifted his shoulders back a touch, then the fight left Pete's eyes. "It's too damn hot to fight, Trigger. We can't wait for the trains, is all I'm sayin'."

Cal nodded and sat back on the flour sacks. "When your brother gets back, Pete, I'll lay it all out. It's too damn hot to say things twice."

Ben produced a pack of cards and started dealing out a game of Pharaoh, which Rubin and Pete joined. Silas let out a disappointed sigh and lowered his hat's brim. Pete was a burr in Cal's saddle blanket, but the shit of it was he wasn't wrong. He needed to find the Six a new job, or they'd turn on him — and pickings were already slim.

Chapter Two

BRYAN CARTER STRODE THROUGH THE BARN DOOR LATER that afternoon with a magazine balanced on a sun-bleached crate filled with dry goods and one bottle of brown liquor.

"That it?" Silas asked.

Bryan didn't answer, just set the crate down and walked around to look at his brother's cards. While Pete was by no means a small man, Bryan had inherited all of their dad's height and brawn. His shoulders cast a shadow over the game and drew an irritated look from Pete.

"You up or down?" Bryan asked.

"What's it matter?" Pete said.

"Just askin' is all."

"If we'd been playing for real, Ben would only be wearing his boots and drawers. Rubin's only still in this because he's cheating."

Bryan put a hand on his bowie knife and glanced at Rubin. "That true?"

Rubin shrugged. "He's only mad because I catch him as much as he catches me."

Pete held up a hand as Bryan stepped to Rubin. "I don't mind that he does. Makes it interesting."

Bryan relaxed. "Suits me, Pete."

Cal nudged the crate with his boot. Sack of flour, spot of rancid-looking butter, wrinkled ham-joint, and a bag of peas. He waved Bryan over. "Thought there'd be more than this."

Bryan shook his head. "Buzby's all picked clean. Said there might be more in Sunset."

"There's a lot more of everything in Sunset," Silas said.

"Including Jedidiah Scott," Ben said.

"Yeah, him, too," Pete said.

Cal picked up the rolled magazine and pulled a stool to a convenient light beam. "I reckon Buzby's hoarding and hoping the railroad gets the bridge fixed later rather than sooner. I'll cut a deal with him later. He doesn't want Sheriff Scott's attention any more than we do."

Pete cocked his head at the magazine in Cal's hand. "That the *Gazette*? You wanting to know how the ladies are wearing their hair in London or some such?"

Bryan sniggered.

Cal gave a solemn nod. "That might do, Pete. I'd rather think about them than have to look at your ugly faces." He caught a whiff of rancid cheese and pushed Bryan farther away. "Like to think they smell prettier, too."

"Let me know if you find something interesting," Silas said.

"Not you, too," Pete said.

Silas grinned. "Might help with the sportin' ladies. Never know, might get a discount."

"They don't care what you talk about, so long as you don't have empty pockets. Better not to talk at all, I say," Pete said.

"No wonder the last one run off. You probably bored her to death," Rubin said. He closed his eyes and let out a snore. Silas cackled as did Cal. Bryan even cracked a smile.

"It's the train schedules," Ben said quietly.

Cal tapped his head and pointed to Ben before rifling through the *Gazette* and folding its pages back. His finger ran down the tables. "We got the Wichita Flyer passin' through Friday evening. Likely have a few trail-tired cowboys taking the easy way back."

"And probably spent all their money as soon as they got paid out, only enough left for the train," Silas said. "Did that myself more times than I can count."

"Sounds about right," Bryan said.

"There's the express out of Kansas City, might be worth it," Ben said.

"Have to hit it in Comanche Country," Rubin said. "Too dangerous."

Pete leaned back from the card game and read over Cal's shoulder. "There's an odd gap between Youngstown and Denver. Might be hiding a payroll run to the Houghton mines."

"If there a train, it'll be watched over by more than dregs. Pinkertons, even," Ben said.

"We can take 'em," Pete said.

Cal shook his head. "Not without killing a few."

"Maybe we need to stop worrying about killing a few folks standing between us and our money," Pete said.

"No, that'll just bring 'em down harder and put a bigger price on our heads," Cal said.

Pete tapped his cards against the tabletop. "The Crows don't have that problem."

Ben nodded. "And they're part of the reason we have to worry about Pinkertons in the first place. We had a nice thing going until they moved in."

"What about the 1:30 to Albuquerque?"

"The 5:35 Union Pacific outta Springfield…"

Cal shook his head. From what he knew about the trains they could hit, most would either be poor pickings or too dangerous to take. Maybe San Francisco wasn't such a bad idea after all. He turned the page and creased the magazine back as he scanned the westbound lines.

"What if we picked up stakes and hit the Wilson line in Nevada? Then up to the Carson Run so they think we're heading Oregon way, but we cut straight west?"

Pete threw his cards down. "We got a good thing going here, Trigger. Why mess that up?"

"Best way to keep trouble from finding you is to keep moving sometimes."

Silas turned his head sideways and read the page facing away from Cal. "What about that?" Silas said.

"About what?" Cal said. He realized Bryan's bored look had evaporated at Silas's discovery, and the big man was licking his lips as he read. Cal turned the *Gazette* over. CARPATHIAN RELIC MAKES JOURNEY TO NEW WORLD.

"That's the fanciest coffin I ever did see," said Bryan.

"That's not a coffin, it's a sarcophagus," Ben said.

"What's a sar-cough-august?" Bryan said.

"It's a fancy coffin," Ben said.

Bryan's eyebrows beetled. "That's what I said."

Pete's eyes lit up. "Yeah, but sarcophagus is an old word, a fancy word. And when I think of old and fancy, I think of rich people." He waggled his eyebrows, and Cal felt the others press closer.

"Says here the historic artifact is on its way to a museum in San Francisco where it will be studied by the illustrious Professor Gregory Talbot. He looks well enough off to me. Reckon we can fetch it for him and see how much this high-falutin' body box is worth to him," Pete said.

"Are we that low, Pete? Grave robbing?" Cal asked.

Pete put his arm over Bryan, who was still mouthing the words as he read, and stuck a finger in Cal's face. "There's no risk of killing the mark. He's already dead, right? And who hires Pinkertons for a casket? It's as close a peach as we'll ever see."

"Seems like borrowing trouble," Cal said.

"You suddenly find religion?" Pete asked.

Cal kept his hand from reflexively touching the crucifix. "It just doesn't seem right."

"We've taken a widow's last penny, Cal," Ben said. "If you can make peace with that, you can make peace with this."

"But how much is it really worth? Looks like a stone coffin to me. Heavy. Won't fit in your saddlebags, so you'll need a wagon to haul it. A slow wagon. And it don't spend like money or gold. If this Professor won't pay, where are we gonna unload it? There's gotta be something better."

Bryan finished reading and looked up. "So it's old?"

Pete rolled his eyes. "Have you not heard what I just said?"

"Like conquistador old?"

"Older than that, I reckon," Pete said.

Bryan nodded. "I know this dipshit in Montana name of Callahan that paid a hundred dollars for a rusty conquistador helmet. Cattleman's son, got a mansion up in Montana territory he's filling with old shit like that. If a rusty bucket is worth a hundred, that fancy coffin gotta be worth at least a thousand to him, right?"

Ben read on. "It's taking the Butcher Trail."

"How you figure that?" Cal asked.

Ben tapped the *Gazette's* date at the top of the page. "Last month it was in Parker's Butte. Would have taken the train right through Sunset, but…"

"But the bridge washed out over Chorizo Gorge," Pete said.

"So it's either backtrack to Denver and add another month, or you hire a wagoner to take it on Butcher's Trail to the station in Youngstown."

Rubin got a far-off look. "Maynard's Pass?"

Silas clucked his tongue. "Maynard's Pass."

"It's perfect," Pete said.

Cal reached into his pocket and adjusted the cross poking into his stomach. He shook his head. "Bad medicine."

"You wanna keep eating weevil-infested johnnycakes and cracking your teeth on dried peas all summer? It's the easiest money we'll ever make, Trigger," Pete said.

"Maybe we could hit a bank, a small one," Cal said.

Pete gaped. "You just said—"

"Or that mining office in Youngstown," Cal said.

"They're even worse than the banks. They hire on all the regulators the railroads fire for killin' too many Chinese and Irish," Silas said.

Rubin looked up at Cal "It is good score, *ja*?"

Bryan nodded. "Just take it to Dipshit, Montana. He won't even ask. By the time we circle back, the bridge'll be fixed and maybe it won't be so blazin' hot."

Cal looked at the men's faces and knew he was beat. The job made sense, a lot of sense. His gut told him this wasn't a good idea, but it also told him that if he fought the others on this, he'd lose them to Pete, and that would get them all killed.

Cal's hand slipped into his pocket and touched the calico for luck. He rolled up the *Gazette* and summoned a grin. "Fine. Round up the horses. We ride out tonight, boys."

Chapter Three

NED WATERBY HUNCHED OVER THE REINS AND KEPT HIS eyes fixed a few yards ahead of the team. The trail through the scorched wilderness of Maynard's Pass had seen better times, and it wouldn't do to have the wagon's wheel break from a stuck rut or hidden boulder. He feared if that happened, not only would his men leave him, but the horses might, too. Then he'd be alone, just him and the cargo. It shifted and scraped against the wagon's wooden bed with every rock, ditch, and bump, and the men, Ned included, shifted with it, pushed and pulled in their seats like flies in a spider web.

Ned adjusted his hat against the noonday sun, blinked the trail dust from his eyes, and steered the team around a protruding rock he didn't like the look of. Carl shifted on the bench next to him, reaching out and touching the shotgun butt jutting from the wagon's built-in at his knee. Carl was whispering to himself and had been for the past two days. The others weren't much better off, with Tom head down and absently scratching his arm raw, and the kid, Jasper, twitching his head all bird-like in every direction except at the lump under the wagon's tarp.

For himself, a tickle had settled in his chest on the first day and been spreading ever since, growing into a racking cough. His throat burned raw and felt crackly with each inhale, but so long as it wasn't the consumption, he'd endure it. He had no choice.

Carl's muttering stopped, and Ned spared a glance his way. Carl seemed surprised himself. The wagon rocked over an old rut, and the scrape of stone over the wagon's iron-banded wheel sent a shiver down Ned's back. Carl also flinched, then looked away, shaking his head and resumed whispering to himself.

Ned knew he should look back over his shoulder and ensure the cargo was still tied down securely, but he couldn't bring himself to. It was fine. Surely it was fine. And if it wasn't, it was someone else's turn to cinch the ropes tighter. That's what he had hired them for, anyway, though he supposed he was getting what he paid for. What he'd scraped and saved his whole life for amounted to a rickety wagon, a few supplies, and three men who brought their own guns and would work for next to nothing. But that wasn't important. What was important was to get the cargo to Youngstown on time and collect the payout. Then he'd get the next contract, and the next until his shipping business was more than just himself and a rickety wagon, growing into a bustling empire of its own.

His dreams of empire kept his mind off his cough. The trail dropped into a little slot canyon which gave blessed relief from the sun. The horses at least had the sense to stay to the trail's middle as the way wound between scrub patches along the canyon floor, until they bristled and whinnied coming around a bend. Ned brought the wagon up short at a deadfall across the trail.

It wasn't a large tree, but he didn't fancy the wagon's chances rolling over it without breaking a wheel or catching against the axle. Then he spied a pair of boots sticking out from under the trunk. The air wasn't rotten with flies, so whatever happened must have been a spell back.

"Jasper! Go see what happened to that poor soul," Ned said to the kid. Then, figuring Jasper would as likely scare as not, added, "Tom, you back him up."

Jasper hopped off the back of the wagon and adjusted his gun belt, which was always slipping down his narrow hips. Tom did the same, though for the opposite reason. The kid walked forward with the irrational confidence of youth, with Tom lagging behind, stooped.

Jasper's head tilted to the side, bird-like. "I don't—"

The air erupted with gunfire and splitting wood. The horses reared in their harness and jerked Ned forward by the reins. He pulled back instinctively as a bullet buzzed past his scalp. He wrestled with the drive lines, trying to reverse the team and turn the wagon around, but the horses fought each other and ignored his command. He shouted something, he didn't know what, and his right ear went deaf as Carl's shotgun boomed.

Twin geysers exploded from pits on either side of the trail, sending dust billowing through the narrow canyon walls.

Demonic shadows appeared in the dust and moved like lightning, knocking Tom and Jasper to the ground and snatching their guns away. Two more demons rose from the ground and rushed the wagon.

The tangled lines jumped in Ned's hand, and the wagon groaned as the team reared their traces. The wagon lurched sideways and timber snapped like bones breaking. Ned hauled back on the leads and settled the wagon just as a shadow appeared from the corner of his eye and hot metal kissed his temple.

"Put 'em up," the tall demon said. Ned blinked, then he realized the demon was just a man. A scary man, no mistake, with pale eyes above the dust-covered kerchief hiding his lower face, but a man nevertheless. Ned glanced at Carl, and found him possessed by a masked demon of his own, hands in the air and shotgun in the dirt. Ned followed suit.

The outlaw's eyes narrowed, and he backed up a step gesturing for Ned to get out.

"I've got men on the rim with rifles, and another fifteen at both ends of the canyon bottling you up. That's all of fifty, mind, so don't get any ideas."

The bandits were just as quick searching and relieving Ned and his men of coin, jewelry, and pocket watches. One of them, near as big as the leader with dark hair and two bowie knives tucked in his belt, paused as he looked down at Ned's feet.

"Boots off," he said.

Ned had been numb to the whole experience up until that point. The men had his wagon, with the cargo he would never get paid for, his horses, and his last dollar. Now his boots? A man had to stand for something, didn't he?

"I just bought them," Ned muttered.

The outlaw's fist cuffed him behind the ear, rattlesnake-quick. "You fixin' to die over boots?"

Ned blinked away the stars and shook his head. He sat in the dust and levered off his footwear. The bandit held them up to his own feet and grunted. In moments, Ned's boots walked away on the outlaw's feet.

"Can I at least have your old boots?" he called to the outlaw's back.

The man turned around and blinked. "No," he said as if Ned had said the dumbest thing in the world, then mounted the wagon.

"All there?" the leader asked a smaller outlaw wearing glasses, who took a peek under the tarp and nodded. To the bigger man, he said, "Take this heap back around. I'll meet up with you and the others presently."

The outlaw with Ned's boots looked confused for a moment, then nodded and tossed the bag full of wallets, watches, and coin behind the driver's box. A bandy-legged outlaw settled into Ned's old seat next to the spectacled one and took up the leads. He said something in German and clucked his tongue, turning the team around smoother than Ned had ever managed.

Another outlaw with the devil in his eyes disappeared and returned minutes later with a string of horses and murmured something to the leader, who looked at Ned and strode over. The man brushed his duster aside and brought his right hand to the revolver at his hip.

"On your knees," he said.

The others looked to Ned and found himself wishing for a lot of things — most of all, the courage to die standing up. To his shame, he lowered his head and followed the man's orders. The outlaw stepped a circle around them, spurs jangling. Ned's thoughts flew too fast to comprehend, mostly settling on the mistakes he'd made in life and how this one was the biggest.

The jangling stopped, and Ned felt an icy prickling at the back of his head. That's where the bullet would go. Dust caked on his lips, but his dry tongue could only push it around, and he didn't trust his trembling hands to brush it away. He caught the sharp whiff of fresh piss. Maybe it was his own.

The man whistled, then Ned cried out as something

thudded to the ground before him. His eyes focused. Four canteens.

The leader was mounting his horse with the others before Ned found his voice.

"You're not going to kill us?" Ned asked.

The leader shook his head. "Reckon it'll take you a day or two to get back to town, so make the water last. There's a spring five miles back on the east side, so best you not miss it."

He rode off on his Appaloosa, not glancing back. The wagon was already out of sight.

They knelt in the dust for an eternity until the man disappeared. Ned glanced down and was relieved to find his trousers dry.

"Shee-it, it's three day's walk and that's a fact," Jasper said.

Ned hobbled over to the canteen, picking his way over sharp pebbles. He picked up the closest canteen, thankful for its full gurgling weight. The numbness of the attack left him, and he braced for its aftermath. He hobbled farther and reached down to touch his wagon's wheel ruts, then tears began flowing.

A hand squeezed his shoulder. "I'm sorry, Ned," Carl said. "Sorry as all hell. I don't know what it's like to lose everything. I imagine it feels like a hundred kicks to the gut with another hundred on the way. "

"No, it's not like that at all," Ned said.

"Beg your pardon, Ned. Just tryin' to help."

"No, you misunderstand, Carl." Ned could feel the wagon pulling farther and farther away, and as it did, Ned felt lighter. The ache in his bones retreated, and his chest loosened. The dust around them cleared as a breeze shot through the canyon and chilled his sweat-slicked brow while drying the wet fabric between his shoulders. The sun burned hot again, yes, but also cleansing, chasing the last miasma from his thoughts. Ideas and possibilities flowed once again. Ned unscrewed the canteen's top and let the sweet water soothe his parched throat.

Ned raised his arms to the sky and smiled for the first time in months. "Praise be to God, this is the greatest day of my life."

Chapter Four

Pete howled and rushed ahead, tagging his brother's shoulder. Bryan shouted and rode off after him, followed by Silas, whose horse quickly caught up and passed the Carter brothers. The three began weaving between creosote bushes and leaned low in their saddles to knock the tallest blooms from Indian paintbrush and lupine. Ben, riding shotgun on the wagon, whistled after them with a grin on his face before going back to sorting the loot in the gunny sack and counting the money. Next to him, Rubin shook his head and kept a steady hand on the leads, casting a glance over his shoulder as the wagon's floorboards groaned from a small bump on the trail.

"This wagon is shit," Rubin called out.

Cal nodded, not trusting himself not to puke if he opened his mouth. He'd been cold as lake ice at the ambush, but now a tremor danced through his bones and would for the next hour, twisting his guts in knots and keeping his heart racing. He'd learned over the years to keep the sick behind his teeth and stay in the saddle which was good enough to keep the others from poking fun.

Bryan and Pete circled back at a trot, grinning wide and trading punches to the shoulder. Silas rode behind them, seemingly relaxed enough to fall asleep now that he'd won the horse race.

"Hey Bryan!" Silas called.

"Yeah?"

Silas affected a meek stutter. "Can I have your boots?"

"No!" the crew shouted, and the five broke down laughing.

Pete pulled his horse alongside Cal. "How many men you tell him we had, Cal? Fifty?"

"A hundred!" Bryan said.

"Three Comanche war bands," Ben said.

"Apache!" Rubin yelled.

Cal twisted his lips in a grin and shrugged. His old sergeant said the tremors were normal after battle and would soon pass. Cal had meant to ask him if it ever got easier, but the old goat caught a load of grapeshot at Vicksburg before Cal could work up the courage. As the war went on, he discovered the answer himself: it didn't.

Pete pointed to the wagon. "That's got to be the easiest score we ever had. No hero wannabes, no iron lockboxes, no cryin' women."

"That was all my idea, putting the boots under the tree," Bryan said. "Worked like a charm."

Pete nodded. "A fine idea, Bryan. You're not as dim as Ma said. Ow!" Bryan's fist hit Pete's shoulder hard enough to make even Silas wince.

"I don't think I had to reload at all," Rubin said.

"Me neither," said Silas.

"I still have three bundles of dynamite," Ben said with a trace of regret.

"And no one got hurt," Cal said.

"Not even winged," said Pete. "I told ya, Cal."

Cal swallowed back the rising bile and nodded. "You did, Pete."

Pete sat up straighter. "So what'd we take from them boys?"

"About fifty dollars in coin and greenbacks, another twenty once we sell their guns and watches," Ben said.

"Anything worth keeping?" Silas asked.

"Just their food and Bryan's boots." Ben said.

"Damn right," Bryan said. "Don't forget the wagon and horses."

"We'll need those to get to Montana."

"Sure, but after? That's gotta be…"

"Call it 1200 or roundabouts. 200 apiece."

Silas let out a low whistle.

The others devolved into dreaming and lying about what they'd do with their cut, but Cal's mind drifted west, all the way to California and the ocean. His thoughts wandered up the coast, then back east to Montana, and he wondered if it was easier to deal with the winters there than the summers in Sunset Valley.

"What you doing with your cut, Cal?"

Cal blinked, then covered his surprise by rubbing at his jaw and giving the bristly scruff at his chin a good scratch. "I expect like Silas, I'll lose most of it at the card table, a little more to some fine bottles of whiskey, and the rest to all the ladies waitin' to take advantage of me." It got him a few laughs and he smiled along with his crew. He even managed to keep the grin when the wind lifted a corner of the wagon's tarp and he was reminded they were joshing around a dead man's bones. He looked away before his thoughts dwelt on it and further agitated his already sour stomach.

Cal adjusted his hat. "Though it occurs that if we get a good price, might be I stay around Montana after."

Pete looked at him like he'd sprouted horns. "You going soft in the head, Trigger? This was the easiest score we've seen since, well, ever." He looked to Bryan, who nodded along. "Banks? Trains? Forget 'em. Leave 'em to the Crows. It'll be scores like this to keep us flush from here on, right boys?"

Bryan responded with a "hells yeah," which Cal took as a matter of course. He expected the others to have more sense, but their faces reflected Pete's sentiment.

"Think there's a steady stream of rich dead fellas crossing the plains, Pete?" Cal said. "Most people get buried not too far from where they fall along the way."

Pete looked away from Cal with a shrug and focused on the trail ahead. "Don't pretend to be an idiot, Trigger. Montana? Really? With all that snow and shit? You get miserable and ornery with the first frost."

"Maybe we should play out this job first. There's no money in our pockets, just a stone box and a bullet-ridden, busted-ass wagon," Silas said.

Ben nodded. "Play it out, see what happens."

Bryan spat. "Pete's right. I ain't gonna get shot at for pocket watches and wallets no more."

"I hate snow," Rubin muttered.

The trail forked, and they drifted left to the spur that would take them back to Sunset Valley. Cal enjoyed what was left of the breeze before the left turn would take him off the high prairie and back into the twisted folds of Sunset Canyon. He felt the urge to just take his cut now and go right or turn around entirely. The stone box in the wagon felt like it was tied around his neck and he was about to be thrown in the ocean. He could make it work in Montana, snow be damned. He'd figure it out. He had a good horse in Rocky, his paired Navy .36s, and a bedroll. Cal had cut and run before with less to his name.

But if he did, what would happen to his crew? Pete, that's what. He and his big dumb brother would lead the others in some damned foolish job and get shot up or caught. They might not even get that far. It'd might be that Pete would shoot off his mouth and one of the others, likely Silas, would shoot back with his Colt. It'd all go to hell from there. All because Cal felt a little queasy about robbing a dead fella?

He'd kept these men together, bled for them. They were a sorry bunch, but they were his sorry bunch. Leaving now would be nothing less than an act of cowardice.

Cal nudged Rocky to the left. "You're probably right, Pete. The cold never did a man no good."

Pete sat up straighter in the saddle. "I know I'm right, Trigger. That's why you keep me around."

Chapter Five

THE BOTTOM OF SUNSET CANYON WAS FILLED WITH THAT infernal kind of trail dust that turned men and horses into pale ghosts and covered deep ruts for wagon wheels to discover and crash against. Cal blinked against the sweat trickling through his eyebrows and worked the broken branch between a rock and the wagon's jammed wheel.

"Three ... two ... one ... yah!" Cal set his shoulder and heaved with the others while Rubin coaxed the team forward. Wood groaned, then something snapped. Cal's stomach twisted for a moment. He thought it was the wheel snapping, or worse, the axle, but the wagon shifted and bounded forward.

"Damn, my boots!" Bryan said.

"Get your toes?"

"Did I say my toes?" Bryan stooped and shook his head. "Split the damn leather."

"You're lucky," Rubin said.

"Lucky I don't knock a couple teeth out your mouth."

Rubin dusted his hand off and looked down from the

driver's seat. "You're welcome to try, you don't mind losing a few yourself."

"Cut it out," Cal said. "We still got a long way to go. You two feel like fighting when we're back at the ranch, I won't stop you."

"Makes more sense to stop now," Pete said and pointed. "That stand of trees will do us just fine, and we'll still make it back before sundown tomorrow."

Cal shook his head. "We go another hour or two, we can make it tomorrow morning before the heat sets in."

Pete leaned in and lowered his voice. "Bryan ain't gonna make it that long. You know what he's like once he gets a notion in his head. It'll stew, Cal. Let him cool down and he'll be back to his cheery self come morning."

Cal looked to Ben, who blew out a long breath and heaved the broken branch aside. "It's been a long day, Cal. We got this shitbox wagon through the worst of it, but we don't know how tough these horses are that been pulling it. What're the chances that bootless wonder got top stock for his penny-ante operation?"

"Ben's got a point, Cal," Pete said.

Cal briefly missed his army days where he could have just ordered his men to do as he said. He wasn't a soldier anymore, he reminded himself. He could only push his crew so hard, even when it was for their own good.

Cal pointed Rocky towards the trees. "Fine. But we're getting up at first light."

Bryan and Rubin were still at each other after they made camp.

"You been riding that wagon all day, Rubin. Some of

us had to actually work today." Bryan plopped himself down on the ground and shook off a boot.

"Not my fault. Not cooking. Not getting *vater*."

"Wah-ter, you foreign fuck. Wah-wah-wah-ter."

Rubin didn't give any warning, he just launched himself at Bryan and took the bigger man by surprise, driving him to the ground and getting two solid licks into the ribs and face before Bryan hooked Rubin's elbow and rolled him to his back. Bryan pushed his forehead into Rubin's temple, which Cal knew from personal experience hurt like hell even if it didn't do much damage. Rubin keened and flailed, but his fists only glanced off Bryan's meaty shoulder and back, doing no damage. Bryan's follow up, a hammer fist to Rubin's breadbasket, was a different story. Rubin's wail was cut short as the wind rushed out of him, replaced with gasping.

"Reckon that's enough," Cal said.

Pete and Ben waded in and pulled Bryan off. Rubin rolled to his feet and sipped at the air, trying to get his body to remember how to breathe. Ben brought him up to his feet and kept him steady. Bryan gathered himself like he was going to start a second round but stopped when Silas stepped in the middle.

"All y'all are like a bunch of old women sometimes," Silas said. "All this squawking and kicking up dust is starting to get a might aggravating."

"I'm surprised your lazy ass is even up, Silas." Pete held out a hand to Bryan, who ignored it and rose under his own power, dusting himself off. He looked past Silas's shoulder and gave Rubin a blood-smeared grin.

Silas shrugged and nodded to where he'd tied off the horses. "My job's done already. Fixing now to take a nap, but who could with all this racket about?"

"Half-assed as usual," Pete said and pointed to the

team still hitched to the wagon. "What about them? You such a piss-poor cowboy you can't deal with a wagon harness? Do you need me to teach you?"

"That's enough, Pete," Ben said. "We're all tired."

Silas grinned. "Yeah, Pete. We're all tired of your yapping."

Pete swung at Silas, who stepped aside and put a boot across Pete's ankle. Pete tumbled in a dust cloud. Silas turned just as Bryan lowered a shoulder and sent Silas to the ground. Rubin surged forward, but Ben held him back as Cal stepped in.

Cal caught Pete by the collar and shoved him into his brother, then headed off Silas. The kid's eyes danced, and Cal could see him figuring the odds until Cal put a hand on his gun.

"I'm callin' it," Cal said.

Pete wiped a spot of blood from his lip and started to say something, but Cal held up a finger and stared him down.

"Listen," Cal said.

"Listen to what?" said Pete. He touched under his nose and grimaced at the blood on his fingertips.

Cal let the silence hang, then let his eyes drift aside and into the sky before refocusing on Pete.

"I don't hear nothing," Bryan said.

"Exactly. Not even the bugs are buzzing."

"So?" Bryan asked.

Cal frowned and turned his attention to his crew. "So I don't like it. Something's spooked the critters around here, and it's not from you tussling. So button it up and keep an eye open."

Pete wiped at the blood trickling from his nose and lip and scowled at the smears across his hand. "You want to move camp, Trigger?" he asked.

Cal shook his head. "No, this is good ground, and it's already getting dark. Go help Rubin with the wagon. Silas and Bryan can unhitch and settle the team. Ben, start the fire, I'll get us some more wood."

The six split and went about getting the camp set up with only the usual amount of cursing and complaining. Rubin and Bryan still shot ugly looks at each other, but they stuck to their jobs. Cal searched the area for wood, which took longer than it should have and only yielded a meager armful of scrub and tinder. He didn't like all the places he spotted that could hide a group of men and their horses but liked the idea of riding out and scouting in the fading light even less. The camp's sight lines and Mister Winchester's rifles would have to do for now.

Cal stomped back into camp, where Silas and Bryan were checking over the unhitched wagon nags, and Ben was on his hands and knees coaxing a flickering flame in the fire pit. Pete wrestled and swore at the ropes securing the wagon's tarp. He was still dabbing gingerly at his face and wiping the blood on the sarcophagus.

"Pete, don't get any blood on the merchandise." Cal pointed at the partial bloody handprints on the carved stone.

Pete took a look and waved a hand. "Been in the dirt for a hundred years, it oughta be able to take a little blood. I mean, it's already dirty, right?"

"Just that much more to clean up when we try selling it."

"I don't know, Trigger, maybe it'll just add to its value, you know?"

"Quit bleeding on it, all I'm saying." Pete got that look he did when digging in for an argument, so Cal left him alone. He dropped off the wood and when he looked back at the wagon a few minutes later, Pete was walking away, the blood splatters gone. He hadn't expected Pete to give in and clean up his mess that quickly.

"Huh," Cal said. Ben looked up with raised eyebrows. "Nothing," Cal replied to the unspoken question. "Thought I had Pete all figured out, but I guess I didn't."

Chapter Six

Alton Blackfeather waited until the shadows fell across the Wild Six's camp. He counted heads. Trigger Jones. The Carter boys. Silas Beasley. Ben Horn. That kraut Bauer. The whole gang. Dumb name, the Wild Six. More fitting for an outfit that cheated at cards or held tent shows for gawking city tenderfoots. Didn't mean they weren't dangerous if they should happen to spot him peeking through the scrub grass, so Alton endured the biting flies and dripping sweat while he watched and puzzled out what those idiots had on their shot-up wagon.

Gold? Guns? Dynamite? Hopefully not dynamite. Like as not, one stray bullet would send everything sky-high, which would solve the problem of how to separate the Six from their loot, Alton supposed, but it'd piss off Crazy Eye. Or maybe it wouldn't. The Crows would miss out on the score, but they wouldn't be scrappin' with the Six all over the valley, either.

Alton reckoned he had a handle on the camp and eased himself through the scrub on his elbows and belly to a washout and quick-timed it back to Crazy Eye and the rest of the Dust Crows.

ALTON JUMPED down into a dry riverbed and patted the powdery dust from his clothes. Men lined the depression, fanning themselves with hats while trying and failing to keep heat at bay, not to mention the concentrated reek of sweat, gunpowder, and horses in too tight a space. Alton could taste it all at the back of his tongue, which was why he'd made Crazy Eye keep the rest of the Dust Crows well downwind of the Six's camp, as well as staging a canteen so he could grab a quick swig of alkaline water before reporting to his boss.

Crazy Eye sat like a cockeyed toad on his camp stool, fingers clasped across his belly, tin cup perched on his knee. Alton swore the funny eye always saw him first, and then decided whether or not to let the rest of Crazy Eye ken to what was going on. This time, the eye decided it was too busy, and the boss jerked as Alton approached, nearly knocking the cup to the ground.

"Where are they?" he grunted.

"Right where you said they'd be," Alton said. "Just the six of 'em, their horses, and a shot-up wagon with a big box, looks heavy."

Crazy Eye drained the cup and smacked his lips. "Just as it should be." He levered himself out of the camp stool and bellowed. "Crows! Time to get ours." The other Dust Crows gathered around, dirty and scraggly in Alton's mind, eighteen men half feral from months of heat and poor eating. Crazy Eye turned to fix each one with his off-eye as he spoke. "Pair up and circle 'round the camp, quiet-like. I want pairs coming from each compass point."

He jabbed a finger at two Crows holding buffalo rifles. "You two creep up the east hill and rain down hellfire."

"Watch your feet, there's a lot of loose scree there," Alton said.

Crazy Eye nodded. "Wait until the rest of us move in before you start firing. We don't need another fuckup like last time. Right, Rory?" He fixed the rifleman with his off-eye.

Creeping Rory squirmed. "My finger slipped."

"Is it going to slip again?"

"No, Crazy Eye."

"Make sure it don't. Else I'll have Mumbles cut it off."

Mumbles, a small man with streaks of gray in his hair, didn't look up at his name, but let his hand drift to the Arkansas Toothpick at his belt. Alton and the others had once seen Mumbles drive the blade, closer to a sword than knife in Alton's reckoning, clear through a man and cackle at its bloody tip like a kid with his first jack-in-the-box.

"We sure about this, boss? Something don't feel right, like Trigger is setting us up." The former ranch hand-turned horse thief, Harold, twisted a bandanna in his hands. Alton wondered the same himself. It wouldn't be the first time Trigger Jones and the rest of the Six turned the tables on the Crows.

Crazy Eye rounded on the man. "You scared, Harold? You dribbling in your breeches already?"

Harold's face flushed as he shook his head. "No, Crazy Eye. I ain't scared."

"Anyone else?" Crazy Eye asked. "I won't have geldings in this outfit. No? All right then. Move out, wait for the signal."

The Crows split, leaving Alton to follow Crazy Eye through the scrub.

"I didn't want to say it in front of the men, boss, but Harold ain't wrong. Something's not right about this." He rushed his words before Crazy Eye could blow up. "Why were they so easy to track? Why now?"

Crazy Eye paused, then tapped his nose and pulled at his earlobe. "I can smell the money. I hear it jingling on the wind, same as ol' Trigger. It's got a pull on him powerful enough to coax him out from that hideout where they're all buried like ticks on a hound. We've bled him though, Alton. Just enough he got desperate for a score. We faced some lean days ourselves, but it'll all be worth it. After tonight, the Crows will have the valley all to ourselves. To say nothing of the prize on that wagon."

Alton grinned. "Makes it like we're getting paid to wipe them out."

"Like the man said, 'two birds, one stone.' "

"What you figure they found on that wagon?" Alton asked.

"It don't matter. It'll be something worth it. For all his cowardly ways and womanly face, Trigger always could pick the juiciest berry from the bowl."

They arrived at Alton's blind and settled in to give the others time to circle around and get in position. It had been full dark for an hour, and the Six were gathered around the campfire.

"What do you see?" Crazy Eye asked.

"There's no one keeping watch," said Alton.

"Good."

A few minutes later, a shadow flickered near the wagon and slipped out into the night.

"Someone just left camp."

Crazy Eye drew a knife and gave it a practiced flip. The blade wasn't as impressive as Mumble's Arkansas

Toothpick, but Alton knew Crazy Eye kept it sharp enough for shaving. "Probably left to go take a dump," he chuckled. "We'll take him first."

Chapter Seven

Cal kept his eyes fixed on the hills, wishing the moonlight was just a touch brighter. Something had caught his eye a few minutes ago. An animal? Maybe coyotes, maybe not. The air felt heavy and cloying; it would be rough sleeping tonight, assuming he would sleep at all. Dark thoughts had come with the setting sun, setting him maudlin and irritable as the shadows closed in and chased visions of San Francisco away. The men's constant sniping hadn't helped his mood either, setting him on a slow boil until he had to get up and walk out here with his Winchester searching for fresh air. And now this.

He let his eyes play over the hills again, trying to sense the weight of the shadows and find that animal. It had slipped once and sent rocks tumbling downslope. If it would only do it again, he'd be able to spot it in an instant.

He should have fought Pete harder and kept them moving, he realized. The copse of trees and the slight rise of the land meant their camp wasn't completely exposed, but it was a fig leaf's protection if anything serious came their way.

The bushes rustled behind him. It had to be Bryan. Only two on the crew would sneak up on him like that, and Silas was asleep already, like as not. If he looked back now, the campfire would ruin his night vision. "There's something in the hills, Bryan."

Two footsteps, but the cadence was wrong. Cold raced down Cal's spine, and he turned, knowing it was too late. He looked down a pistol's barrel, darker than the night sky. Behind it, a dirty cockeyed man in a blue checked shirt smiled.

"Evening, Trigger."

"Crazy Eye."

"You know, I thought about this moment a lot. Now that it's here —"

A cloaked shadow appeared behind Crazy Eye and fell upon him. Crazy Eye's cry lasted all of an eye blink before a wet crunch and hissing gurgle replaced it. Iron filled Cal's nostrils, and he shuffled back from the dark pool spreading from Crazy Eye's body. Bryan stood and adjusted his duster.

"I don't know about coyotes, but looks like there might be a few dusty crows about," Bryan said.

Cal tugged his hat's brim. "Obliged, Bryan."

Bryan nodded and wiped his bowie knife on Crazy Eye's shirt before turning and disappearing back into the shadows. It wasn't right, a man that size able to move that quiet, but Cal put it from his mind and turned back to the hills, bringing the rifle to his shoulder. He'd lost a bit of night vision, so he had to guess where the not-coyote might set up for shooting down on the camp.

Behind him, the air started cracking with gunshots. The familiar coolness of battle washed down his limbs. Cal sent his own bullet into the hillside, and a moment later saw a flash to the left of his aim, and another flash further yet beyond. At least two coyotes, then.

Cal nodded to himself and brought fingers to his lips. He sent three sharp whistles and glanced back at the camp. Ben was mounted and already heading his way, bent low over the saddle, legs forward of bulging panniers. Cal pointed to the hills.

"At least two more in the rocks where the trail empties out!"

Ben nodded and set the spurs. His horse whinnied and galloped into the night.

Cal sent another two rounds into the hills to keep the bandit's heads down, then turned to see what was going on in the camp. The Crows were coming from the south and east, trying and failing to close the distance between them and his men. Thank the Lord for morons, Cal thought. Assaulting on foot, uphill, with a bright ol' campfire ruining their night vision.

Rubin's repeater barked in measured cadence, the German braced behind the wagon and sent bullets down-range like it was target practice. Silas whooped and rode into the night, a pistol in each hand.

More muzzle flashes, this time from the north. Maybe Crazy Eye hadn't been as stupid as he looked. Cal ran to a rock and steadied his rifle. Two Crows scurried out from some scrub and Cal squeezed the trigger. The man on the right fell. His buddy skidded and started to run back before changing his mind and turning once again. His indecision was all Cal needed. His Winchester bucked, and the Crow fell not two steps from his friend. Cal rolled to the side and started reloading.

He spotted two more Crows charging the camp and took aim just as Bryan emerged from bush, knife rising and falling. The other Crow whirled, only to get shot in the back by Pete. More Crows broke from cover with Silas's horse thundering behind them, quickly finding themselves caught in a crossfire with Pete and Rubin before them and the charging Silas behind.

A bullet from the hillside whizzed by Cal's ear and he dropped. A few of the smarter Crows opened up from the south, and soon the air was filled with bullets, more incoming than outgoing. Pete and Rubin crouched under the wagon, which was adding to its collection of bullet holes. Stone chips flew from the sarcophagus. Cal kept moving, and firing, trying to distract the Crows on the hillside while not exposing himself to a crossfire from the south.

Ben's horse reared and Cal fired into the hills, to give his man time to do his thing. Ben's arm shot forward and a tumbling bundle arced into the rocks above, followed by a second, third and fourth. Ben pulled his horse around and took off at a sprint. A flash lit up the hillside with the rumble reaching Cal seconds later. Rock soared into the air, and for a moment the bandits in the hills must of reckoned Ben's dynamite had missed. But the former railroad man knew his craft, and the rumbling only grew louder as the scree shifted. The hillside fractured and crumbled, rocks flowing like water and crashing against the boulders the Crows were using for cover. The ground under Cal's feet shook, and it occurred to him that Ben might have overdone it as the rocks plowed along, gathering speed and tumbling onto the trail.

Cal shook himself and returned his attention to the camp. Silas ran down another Crow, but his buddy escaped into the brush, Pete's bullets nipping at his heels and elbows. The fight left the others as well, and soon the night air was quiet again but for the tinkling of rocks settling on the trail behind them.

Sunset Blood

Cal let out a breath and promptly threw up.

Chapter Eight

"I KNOW YOU LIKE YOUR DYNAMITE, BEN, BUT GOOD Lord," Silas said.

Ben rubbed the back of his neck and wore a bashful smile. "It never hurts to make sure."

In the morning light, they discovered the rockslide had buried more than just the Crows hiding in the hills. Dirt, boulders, and uprooted trees filled the canyon trail several feet deep.

Cal missed the campfire already. Their camp was still in the ridgeline's shadow and the meager dew left everything he touched sticky and chill. Cal discovered a new hole in his boot as the damp crept in under the ball of his foot.

"We're not getting a wagon over that," Pete muttered. "I wouldn't give you a plug nickel's bet that your horse wouldn't snap a leg, trying to pick through that mess."

"Maybe Rubin knows how to hitch up mountain goats and get them pulling together," Bryan said.

"Knock it off, this is serious," Pete said.

"It'll be fine," Silas said. "We'll just have to hole up a bit longer until it's cleared."

"And how long will that take?" Pete said.

Silas shrugged and looked at Ben, who said, "Four days, if it were a railroad crew. Longer, maybe."

Cal spat, the sour taste in his mouth refusing to fade even after long droughts from his canteen. He breathed deeply to keep his bile where it belonged and not across the scrub where everyone would see it. In the aftermath, he realized leaving the Six back at the trail split would have been a cowardly mistake. Without him, the sniping and vexation might have left them distracted and gotten them all slaughtered in Crazy Eye's ambush. No, they still needed him around.

The blocked pass was a problem, but Cal was more worried about the bodies. He'd seen his share of death and its corrupting effects on a body hours, days, sometimes weeks after the heart beat its last. Union or Confederate, didn't matter, neither did death's instrument, whether musket ball, canister shot, bayonet, or steel-shod hooves. Flesh followed nature's schedule, growing cold, stiff, then settling for a spell before bloating and blackening in the sun. The stench of corruption had never left his memory, and this morning it was all around him, the dead Crows skin as black as coal, blowflies swirling in the air like smoke.

"It ain't right," Cal said. "They look four days gone, not four hours."

"The Reaper's hungry, is all, maybe greedy, too." Bryan said. He spat on the dead Crow. "There, a little something to help him wash it down." He clapped Cal's shoulder. "You sore about something, Trigger? I know you ain't sorry about these Crows. They had it coming."

Cal shook his head and settled himself. Dead was dead, but he had bigger problems. He turned from the corruption and narrowed his eyes as he looked over the blocked trail. "Blocked canyon. Dead bodies. Going to draw attention we don't need. Maybe enough to make a sheriff or marshal decide to take more than a passing interest."

"We could move the bodies," Bryan said. Rubin and Silas exchanged a look that wasn't squeamish so much as grim disgust.

"They're fit to burst," Silas said. "You go first, Bryan, see how long them new boots stay new."

"No time," Rubin said. "They'll have heard the dynamite in Sunset and sent someone to take a look."

"Thanks a lot," Pete said to Ben. "Now we're penned in until they get it cleared, and we're not gonna get paid while we're stuck."

Ben took off his hat and worked a crease out of the brim. "Next time, you can go after the snipers, and I'll tuck in behind the wagon."

"It's not like the coffin will go bad and fall apart," Silas said. "Unlike that wagon. Let it go, Pete, it wasn't going to make it to Montana anyhow, and we'd as likely as not wasted a month along the way replacing the wheels and axles one by one if we tried. We can scrounge up a better one in the next couple weeks."

Pete shook his head. "I want my money now, not months from now. How long we gonna be eating dry beans and biscuits, Trigger? Ain't you worried?"

Cal looked at the coffin's fresh bullet holes and shook his head. "I wonder how Crazy Eye and his raggedy operation was onto us so quick."

"Maybe they got wind of it," Ben said.

"How the hell would he? Even we didn't know what we were up to until the notion struck," Silas said.

"Maybe that wagon's crew got to a telegraph office," Ben said.

Pete choked back a laugh. "And telegraphed Crazy Eye?"

Ben spread his hands. "I don't know, just saying."

"Maybe Ben got up to his old tricks," Pete said to his brother. "Except this time we're the railroad, and the Crows are the ones paying for secrets before he throws us over and joins them."

Ben went still. "I've got no reason to sell you out."

"You sure?" Pete asked.

Ben's arms dropped to his sides, hand drifting to his Smith & Wesson. "Not 'til now. You calling me a liar?"

"You sure are free and easy when it comes to making accusations. Some might say it's a guilty conscious," Silas said to Pete.

Pete took a step forward. "Fuck you, Silas. And while I'm at it, fuck you, too, Ben. Man is what he's always shown, given enough time."

Silas hooked his thumbs in his gun belt. "On that, Pete, you and I agree."

Cal cleared his throat. "Quit hacking on Pete, Silas. He knows damn well there's no way Ben could have snuck off and told anyone what we were up to. Crazy Eye may be a worthless piece of shit, but he's always had a rat's cunning for shiny objects that don't belong to him. I wouldn't put it past him to have a Crow or two tailing us just so they can catch our scraps."

Cal tilted his head towards the dead Crows. "But we showed him, didn't we?"

The others agreed; Bryan, Silas, and Ben with grins, Rubin and Pete not so happy but nodding along with the others, which was good enough for Cal.

"Fact is, we can't stick around. If someone eyeballs our

shot-up wagon, word will get out. Other lowlifes might spook if they don't want to end up like the Dust Crows, but there's always some piss-for-brains that'll come try us."

"Bounty hunters?" Rubin asked.

"Maybe."

"We could try taking it south and around," Pete said.

"A summer ride through the desert? At least you'll have a casket handy, assuming you don't mind sharing with its current occupant," Silas said.

Bryan kicked at the air. "Nah, just kick his bony ass out, I say."

Pete banged a fist against his leg. "Fine. But by the time the pass is clear, word will be out, one way or another. Lord knows who'll be looking for a bunch of cowboys with a fancy coffin. Might be that we just have to take a peek inside and see what we can carry out on horseback for now. Yeah, maybe just whet the appetite of moneybags in Montana for more. This could work, so let's get moving."

"What about the bodies?" Ben asked.

Pete wrinkled his nose. "Leave 'em. Give whoever comes looking something to wonder about." He held up a hand to Cal. "No, I get it, Bryan and I will make it look like Comancheros did this. Scalp a few, slice some ears off, stuff Crazy Eye's pecker in his mouth and such. Then anyone interested will start looking at them and not us.

Cal didn't like it, but he liked staying out in the open less, especially if someone from Sunset was on the way. He especially didn't like the way Bryan didn't mind his brother's plan and wasn't squeamish about his own part in it. The Comanchero angle might work, if whoever came across the bodies had a poor opinion of them, and most around the territory did. Never underestimate a man's ability to swallow a lie he wants to believe.

"Fine," Cal said. "Let's get the wagon rolling, Rubin.

Silas and I will ride point, Ben'll manage the string. Cover our trail best you can but don't lag. I want to be back at the ranch before sundown."

Bryan nodded and started putting on a pair of gloves. "Yeah, and then crack open this stone coffin and see what kind of score we're looking at."

Chapter Nine

It was all Cal could do to stay upright in the saddle, even with the ranch in sight and it being barely into the afternoon. The others weren't much better, too tired from the trail and a lost night's sleep to do more than grunt at each other or stare over their mount's heads. The day's dust and hard saddle made his bones ache and rattle after the thrill of the heist and subsequent ambush had settled. The others looked no better, apart from Silas, who claimed he could sleep with his eyes open, still riding easy and making little jokes. What kept Cal going was the fear one of the men, most likely Silas, would say something and another, most likely Pete, would snap to the idea of retorting with a bullet. But Silas had enough sense not to rib the others overmuch and leave Pete alone altogether.

Cal had thought they'd collapse as soon as they pulled the wagon into the barn, but after putting the horses away and having turns at the water barrel, the Six found new life had returned to their steps as Rubin backed the wagon under cover and tore back the tarp. It was the first time Cal had gotten a good look at the sarcophagus, and even in the barn's dappled light, the stonework was something to behold.

The sarcophagus was long enough to comfortably hold even Cal's tall frame with room to spare, a stone rectangle with carvings on the side depicting a knight doing knightly things: receiving a blessing from a priest, fighting on a battlefield, counseling a king, spreading his hands over a field in blessing, sitting on a throne of his own, though with no crown. Some kind of nobleman for sure, Cal thought. Next to each relief was a panel carved in a language Cal couldn't make heads or tails of.

"Latin," Ben said.

"Can you read it?" Cal asked.

Ben shook his head. "I was never good at it. Would have made a piss-poor priest."

"For more reasons than one," Cal said.

Ben let out a small laugh. "Yes. More than a few." He nodded to the lettered panels. "Near as I can tell this is Lord Braga, and whoever carved all this thought he was one hell of nice feller."

"That's great," Silas said. "But was he rich?"

Rubin brushed fingertips across the carvings. "Not a peasant."

Ben shrugged. "Rich enough not to get dumped in a pine box."

"So that one day he could be abducted by the notorious Wild Six," Pete said.

Bryan laughed, then asked, "What's it say over here?"

Ben craned his neck. "Died in 1259, says some more nonsense, and probably rest in peace at the end."

Silas elbowed Bryan. "How much your pa spend sending you to that fancy school, Ben?" Silas asked.

Ben didn't bother looking up. "More than your pa paid your mother, Silas."

"Don't be too sure. Ma was fancy," Silas replied.

"At least he knows his letters," Pete said.

"That'll come in handy when I pay him to carve your tombstone," Silas said.

Pete gave him a greasy grin. "So long as he spells my name right and doesn't straight-up copy it from yours."

Bryan shouldered his way between the two and placed his hands on the sarcophagus lid. "Let's crack the top and see what's inside." He pushed, but it wouldn't budge, not even when the rest joined in.

"They got him sealed up tighter than Rubin's wallet," Pete said.

"There's no good way to get at it while it's still on the wagon," Ben said, and slumped back. "Put it on the ground and we can get some pry bars and levers on it. "

"Sure you don't want to try dynamite first?" Bryan asked.

Ben cocked an eyebrow. "You want to light the fuse? I promise I won't cut it short, honest."

The longer they stood around the sarcophagus, the more it bothered Cal. They had taken money, watches, jewelry, and lockboxes before. Those were just things. The people they'd taken it from had all left alive, Dust Crows not counting. Nothing they'd taken couldn't be replaced. But the dead couldn't replace anything. Stories of curses and hexes bubbled up in his head. The wrapped cross in his pocket poked him, like it was saying we was in enough trouble already, no need to make a bigger a mistake. "Let's keep the damage to a minimum, yeah?" Cal said. "Maybe we shouldn't open it after all if it's going to be so much hassle. Less risk of breaking something and losing value."

Rubin rocked to his heels. "It already looks like it belongs in a museum. I'd hate to damage it."

Bryan shook his head. "No. You said, Trigger—"

"I know what I said! I'm saying now that I had a ponder on it, and if we're as like to crack the egg before sellin' it, we should leave be."

"That ain't gonna work, Trigger," Bryan said.

"Why not?"

Bryan's jaw worked for a few moments before he turned around and waved his hand. "Tell him, Pete."

Pete glared as his brother but leaned over the coffin. "Even if is worth more in one piece, we should at least know what's in there, or else we're selling a mystery box."

"Could be a lot of shiny in there, could be nothing," Silas muttered.

"Exactly. Maybe not even a body. We gotta know, Trigger. We gotta know if we need to rustle up a corpse to stick in there so Shit-for-Brains Montana is happy."

"So you're fixing to go dig up a grave for real?" Cal said.

Pete spread his arms. "Maybe! Or we'll dump in one of those dead Crows. Crazy Eye for instance."

Cal shook his head. "Ain't no one dumb enough to think that syphilitic sack of crap was some lord from olden times."

"My point is, we don't know, and we gotta. We sell moneybags a pig in a poke, and who knows what he'll do."

"I ain't afraid of no sugar-tit cattleman's son," Cal said.

"You afraid of his money and what trouble it could buy? Bounty hunters? Private posses? Pinkertons?" Pete asked.

"For a coffin?" Ben said.

Pete tapped a finger to his head. "Rich fellas get weird notions. I hope to have a few of my own some day, but I won't — none of us will — without getting the best deal, Cal."

"Still," Rubin said.

"You scared, Rubin?" Bryan said.

Rubin stood and stepped into Bryan's chest. "Say that again."

Bryan smiled and leaned forward. "You heard me."

Cal put a hand on Bryan's shoulder. "Knock it off, you two. Seems to me we aren't of a mind, so let's vote. Do we open it or not? I say no."

"Yes," Pete said.

"Yes," said Bryan, still staring at Rubin.

Ben shook his head. "No."

"Yes," Silas said.

Everyone turned to Rubin. His mouth worked as he held Bryan's stare for another few moments before breaking it for another look at the sarcophagus.

"Papist?" he asked Ben.

"Probably," Ben replied.

Rubin spat on the floor. "Let's see what they buried this asshole with. Be enough to get a bottle of whiskey, yes?"

Bryan slapped Rubin's shoulder. "Maybe two."

Cal swallowed his misgivings and set to work. He knew the stone vault, sarcophagus, or whatever you called it was heavy, but trying to shift it from the wagon was damn near impossible. Curses and disparaging remarks about the carvers' mothers were thrown around, but eventually, Ben and Rubin rummaged around the ranch and rigged up a block and tackle. The barn roof creaked and the whole frame groaned as the sarcophagus finally shifted. For a few gut-wrenching moments, Cal thought the roof would collapse. The vault hung half-on, half off the wagon when the ropes holding it frayed and it dropped to the dirt, but not before clipping the edge of the wagon, smashing through its floorboards and splitting the back axle.

"Damn it all, Rubin, you trying to kill us?" Pete said.

He touched his forehead and came away with a splinter from the wagon.

"If I were, you'd be dead. Unless I were trying to hang you with this crap rope."

"Might need some chains for later," Ben said, duking under a beam.

"New roof, too," said Bryan, brushing splinters and dirt from his face.

Silas crouched and made a show of inspecting the wreckage. "I do believe the wagon's busted," Silas said. "You reckon so, too, Pete?"

Pete's eyes narrowed and his mouth opened, but then he shook his head and turned away. "Forget it. Let's try the lid now."

Silas waggled his eyebrows at Cal as they set pry bars against the lip and heaved. An edge rose. Cal and Ben leaned on their bars while the others pushed from the other side. The stone lid resisted for a moment, then broke loose and slid with a rumble that set Cal's teeth on edge.

Pete let out a low whistle. Cal cursed. Inside the stone vault was another coffin, or more properly, Cal thought, the actual coffin. It was all dark metal, inlaid with silver and gold threads that, through some craftsman's trick, seemed to twist and curl about each other until they came together at the corners to form golden ivy leaves on silver vines. Thick rivets secured the lid, strong as rail ties but ornate enough to be works of art in their own right.

The coffin's lid featured a carved death mask of a man's face with a hatchet nose, heavy brows, and wavy hair that fell past a strong chin. While it could have been an embellishment, Cal thought not; this was what Braga looked like in life. A visage that had inspired men to follow.

"That's a pretty box, ain't it?" Silas said.

"Beautiful," Pete agreed.

"We sure he wasn't a king?" Ben asked.

Bryan clapped his hands and smiled wide. "You know what, boys? I don't know if Montana can afford this. We just might have to find ourselves a buyer who's a little more flush."

Through some rope trick Cal didn't quite follow, Silas and Rubin re-rigged the tackle and hoisted the coffin from the vault. The sides were no less decorated than the top, with more Latin inscriptions, but unlike the stone vault, the carved scenes showed nightmares.

The first panel depicted a gathering of knights around a cave. The second panel showed those same knights underground, armed with swords and short wooden spears battling fanged monsters led by a tall, slender devil. The third panel displayed a slaughter, the knights' bellies gashed open and throats ripped out while the monsters lay dead or dying from spears to the heart or decapitated by the knights' swords. The last panel showed the slender devil getting backed into the coffin by a wounded knight holding a cross.

"That's a hell of a lot of work just to tell a ghost story," Bryan said.

"What you figure, Ben?" Cal asked.

Ben pulled at his lip and shook his head. "I can't make it all out. More Lord Braga and lots of talk about God, the devil, and spirits."

"Superstitious nonsense for scaring peasants," Rubin said.

A shiver tickled the back of Cal's neck, and he twisted it from side to side.

"It don't mean nothing, unless it means it's worth more to some rich church-going type," Pete said. "Though maybe that's not the right play."

"How you figure?" Cal asked.

"Well, how long would it take to find the right man? Rich, pious enough to want this church-y stuff, but not so much that he'd deal with the likes of us."

Bryan's fingers brushed against the ivy, and his knife flashed.

"Watch it," Cal said.

"It's pure!" Bryan said, digging a fingernail into the mark he'd made.

"If we don't want to mess around with finding a buyer, we could just melt it down. It'd spend a lot easier with fewer questions." Silas said.

Ben reached out to touch a metal leaf. "It's worth so much more than that. It'd be like slaughtering a cow for the hock and leaving the steak to rot. This is a rich man's coffin, that's for sure."

"I bet they buried him with jewels," Rubin said.

"Gold rings," Silas said.

"Gold *crown*," Bryan said.

Pete cuffed his brother. "He weren't no king! But he might have something like a fancy snuff box or ivory pipe, or…" He pointed to the carving of the priest backing the devil up. "He might have a nobleman's cross. Wouldn't put it past him to get buried with something holy and expensive in case he had to bribe Saint Peter to get into heaven."

The more they talked, the less Cal liked it. "They could have just buried him in his drawers, too," he said. "These pious types love to seem simple and poor at the end. And what makes you think he's the guy holding the cross?"

Pete snorted. "What, you think he's the monster?"

Bryan laughed, but the others didn't join in, and Pete took offense.

"You're not chickening out now, are you, boys?" Pete asked.

"You gotta admit, that thing makes you feel cold just lookin' at it," Ben said.

Cal agreed. The images on the sarcophagus seemed to twist in his mind when he focused on them for too long. Every detail was beautiful, but the whole was unspeakably ugly and disturbing, as if beauty didn't exist in Braga's time. The dappled afternoon light made the carved devils and tortured knights writhe in shadows. Looking at it filled Cal with a dread he hadn't felt since that black day in the Arizona territory with his Jenny facedown in the dirt, unmoving. He tasted copper at the back of his throat that wouldn't swallow away.

He touched the cross wrapped in its calico and the dread retreated a step back.

"Well, there's an easy way to find out," Pete said. He rapped the coffin's lid three times. "Hello? Anyone home? Any monsters inside?"

The coffin thumped twice.

Pete screamed. Ben and Rubin fell over in a scramble of limbs, and Silas stood frozen to the spot. Cal's gun was in his hand like magic, cocked, and pointed at the coffin.

Laughter filled his ears. Something thumped to the floor and Cal swiveled, gun leading.

He pulled his shot at the last moment, missing Bryan by inches, which just made the man laugh harder. Tears flowed from his eyes and his laugh turned breathless.

Time caught up to Cal and he realized what happened. "You goddamn shit-for-brains! You almost made me plug you!"

Bryan's red face bobbed up and down, unable to speak.

"Not funny," Ben said, which made Bryan laugh all the harder.

"Your … faces!" he managed.

Pete ran over and aimed a savage kick at Bryan's ribs,

but his brother covered up and laughed through three kicks to his meaty shoulder before reaching out and grabbing Pete by the ankle. Pete tried another kick but only ended up hopping off-balance.

Silas unfroze, coughed, and then started laughing himself. Something about it caught on, and soon all the others were laughing along, though Pete's seemed forced.

"Fine, let's set to work," Cal said. "But take care, mind. No sense in breaking things that don't need to be broken."

Cal reloaded his pistol but decided to hang the gun belt on a peg behind him in case Bryan got up to any more antics. His fingertips brushed against the calico in his pocket. That had been too close. With his weapon secured, Cal took up a hacksaw and started in. The saw barely bit into the metal rivet, but it was just a matter of time until he and the others would get through them all, and then they would finally see what all the fuss was about.

Chapter Ten

THE DAY'S SHADOWS HAD GROWN LONG BY THE TIME THE Six had the rivets removed. Cal's shirt stuck to his chest and armpits. His arms and back burned, ached, protested, and then settled into a numb drudgery while the hacksaw had gone dull on his last rivet, and he'd had to muscle through to the end. Still, the long-dead medieval coffin maker had a step on them and his creation fought on, the lid refusing to open. After a careful inspection for latches and hidden catches, Rubin's safecracking skills determined the lid was just plain stuck.

The Six circled the coffin, wedges and pry bars at the ready.

"Take it as easy as you can, boys. A bad slip might take a hundred dollars out of your pocket," Pete said.

Pete counted them off, and they set Pennsylvania steel to gilded iron. Cal leaned into his pry bar, adding more force gently but steady.

"When I kick off, I want something simple," Cal said. "This thing's so tight, Old Braga's soul would never find its way to heaven."

"Assuming he wasn't headed down the other way," Pete said. "Steady, now."

Cal felt the lid tremble, and a moment later it let out a crack like thunder. Dust fell from the rafters, picking out sunbeams lancing through the barn like a heap of pick-up sticks.

"Did something break?" Pete said.

Rubin shook his head. "It's okay. Do not lift further, it slides now like so." He slid his palms against each other, pushing towards Silas and Ben. "You pull, we push."

The coffin lid ground open, and Cal's mind boggled to make sense of the remains inside.

He had been a tall man, Braga, taller than Cal, who never had to bend his neck when looking a man in the eye. The body's clothes and hair had rotted away, and his skin hung in gray stringy tatters over his bones. There wasn't any sign he had been rich, no crown, no jeweled dagger, no gold amulet. Not a single ring on his finger. But that didn't mean there wasn't treasure.

A gold-capped length of wood jutted from Braga's ribcage, inscribed in Latin around a fancy cross. The gold cap was embossed with a seal, a coat of arms with more Latin phrases. It looked heavy enough to crack skulls but had been instead driven through Braga's chest like a spike through a railroad tie.

"Ugly fucker, ain't he?" Silas said and glanced back at the coffin lid with Braga's likeness. "Doesn't look a thing like him."

Pete clicked his tongue. "Beauty's the first to go."

Rubin stared at the wooden spike. "Reckon that's what killed him?"

"Be funny to leave it stuck like that, even if it were," Pete said. "Must be some kind of superstition they had. Like gold coins on the eyes for the ferryman."

"The who?" Bryan said.

"I'll explain it to you later," Pete said.

Silas rubbed his chin and nudged the spike with a finger. "That stake's gotta be worth five hundred just for the gold alone."

"All right, we saw it. Let's seal it back up," Ben said.

"What? After all we went through? Maybe there's more under the bones," Bryan said. He reached for the stake.

The dread Cal put behind him stepped forward. Everything about this thing in its iron box was wrong. He wanted nothing more than to seal the coffin back up and bury it a thousand feet down, but he couldn't explain why. His fingers touched the calico in his pocket, and he thought of someone digging her body up and laying it out in the barn like this, reaching for her…

Pete caught his brother's hand. "Hold up."

"You got a sudden respect for the dead?" Bryan asked.

"I'm just making sure our investment here isn't damaged. Bump that stake and the whole rib cage might shatter. Be worth less."

"Who's gonna know but us?"

"Lay off, Bryan," Cal said. "Seal it back up."

"But we just opened it."

Cal forced a smile. "We can open it later, tonight if you like. I don't know about you, but I'm tired and hungry. Make better decisions and have a steadier hand after a rest and a full belly. And that," he pointed at the body, "is putting me off my supper."

"All right, Trigger," Bryan said.

Cal walked over to help slide the lid back on, but Silas grinned and darted to the stake.

"Catch!" he called out. He yanked the stake from the body, sounding like a knife tearing through old leather. The stake sailed through the air, and Bryan caught it in one hand more out of reflex than trying.

Cal's heart was in his throat, and he found he couldn't breathe. Bryan stood with a dumfounded look on his face while Silas looked on with glee, ready to run if Bryan took umbrage with nearly getting skewered. Then Cal's body remembered how breathing worked, and he pulled himself together. He'd let his imagination turn him yellow, and he didn't have time for that.

Cal stepped between Bryan and Silas before things escalated between the dumbasses. "Dammit, Silas," he said, "How many times—"

The wind kicked up and the barn went cold as if plunged into winter. Oily smoke flowed around them, and someone took in a great choking breath.

Motion. Cal went for his gun, hand grabbing air. *On the peg behind you!* Cal turned for his gun belt, sensing he was already too late.

Torn cloth. Wet splatters behind him. Cal's hand closed on his Navy. He spun, thumbing back the hammer, arm reaching for a target. Silas face-down on the floor. The others standing agog. Wood splintering. An oily black shape climbing up the walls.

He fired and the thing flinched before disappearing into the rafters.

The others were only now reacting, fumbling for their guns.

"Bring it down!" Cal shouted.

They opened up on the shadow within the shadows, Pete and Ben with their pistols, Rubin a moment later with his Winchester, landing hits and making it shudder but hardly slowing it. It twisted around the roof's hole, wisps of white smoke curling whenever the shadow touched the light.

It dropped, hissing as it tumbled through a sunbeam, white and black smoke swirling together. Cal's gun clicked loud in his ears. His arm reached back to his rig on the wall, fingers closing on his second Navy. The shadow stood, and two dim red eyes fixed on Ben. Rubin's repeater cracked, *bam-bam-bam*, bullets sinking into the thing's heart, followed by its head as the shadow sped past Ben, an arm swinging out with a flash of dirty ivory. Ben's head tumbled to the floor, the rest tucked under the shadow's arm as it disappeared up the wall.

Cal fired as more wet sounds reached him, but without effect. The others began pulling more weapons from the wagon as they ran out of ammo. Cal shifted his aim and shot beyond the shadow, punching a hole in the roof behind it. Light hit its back and it screamed. Something fell to the floorboards, and he thought he'd got the bastard until he saw it was just a headless husk wearing Ben's clothes. The shadow faltered as it loped across a rotten roof beam.

Ben's head rolled at Cal's feet, eyes slowly blinking, and for the first time in a gunfight, Cal's stomach heaved. He stumbled as he retched, unable to defend himself, wondering if his head would be next.

Pete hauled back on a dangling rope and whipped the attached tackle pulley into the shadow, knocking it down.

The thing dropped into the sarcophagus, dark smoke coalescing into oily black flesh, red eyes, and bloodstained ivory-taloned fingertips. A mouth full of rattlesnake fangs hissed as it staggered like a drunkard.

Bryan and Pete raised shotguns and hit it high and low. It fell onto its back.

"Close the lid!" Cal shouted.

Rubin was with him, and they heaved. The lid rumbled and Cal's back strained while his boot heels dug into the dirt. A taloned hand caught the lid's edge and shoved back. A second arm emerged and swiped blindly. Talons clawed through Cal's arm, an icy chill followed by searing pain. Its bloody fingers quested further but jerked short as they passed through a sunbeam, setting oily flesh alight with a muffled scream from within the coffin. The free arm jerked, then swiped to the other side and closed around flesh. Rubin flew past him, disappearing into the coffin, boots kicking.

Cal lunged for him but got knocked aside. Pete bashed Ben's feet aside with the butt of his shotgun as Bryan lowered a shoulder and pushed the lid closed.

Cal was on his ass on the floor, staring at Pete. Rubin's muffled screams clawed at the inside of his skull, until the coffin went silent with a single thud.

Chapter Eleven

SHERIFF JEDIDIAH SCOTT PUSHED HIS RANCH BEANS ACROSS the enameled plate with a fork as he watched the drunk cross the saloon floor. The man swayed slightly, smoothing greasy hair against his head before setting his hat at some angle he reckoned ladies couldn't resist. Maybe he thought it made him taller, genteel, or not quite so dirty. The lady behind the bar, his Sarah, wouldn't go for it. She liked her men taller, clean shaven, and plain-spoken. He knew this because she had told him exactly why she had married him when she was pretty enough to have had her pick of dozens of suitors in St. Louis, some of whom could have given her grand houses, lavish wardrobes, and evenings at the theater rather than running a saloon and listening to a lawman's stories of drunks, swaggering railroad detectives, close-mouthed farmers, and the piddly pissant machinations of territorial politics.

She wore her favorite everyday blue cotton dress, which Jed favored as well. She was entering something in a ledger, pen scratching over the paper in what he knew was a neat, precise hand. Her blonde hair was tied back with a black ribbon held by a silver pin which Sarah claimed gave her as much authority in the saloon as his badge did around Sunset. The edges of her hair brushed the back of her neck, making him look forward to helping her let her hair down later and letting its silkiness run through his fingers.

"How much for the hour?" the drunk asked. Jed snapped out of his musings and gripped his fork a little tighter before reminding himself that Sarah dealt with these types all the time. She wouldn't appreciate him stepping in on what she considered saloon business just because he happened to be near. Jed took a slug from his cup and let the acrid coffee war in his mouth with the lingering pepper burn from the beans.

"We've no girls, cowboy," Sarah said.

"Reckon you'll do," he said.

"Do you now?" she said without looking up. "We've got beer, whiskey, vittles, and that's it. You want something more, you'll have to go somewhere else."

The drunk's head lowered, and Jed shifted in his chair, adjusting his hip for easier access to his gun. The drunk took a step forward and said, "There ain't nowhere else."

"There's always Buzby's," she said.

"I like my girls to have all their teeth."

Sarah put down the pen and closed the book before looking up. "And I like my patrons to mind their manners."

The drunk gave her a greasy smile. "I can be nice." He took another step and stopped as a derringer appeared in Sarah's hand. His smile took on a sinister edge. "Now why did you have to go and do that? A peashooter like that is only going to make me ornery."

"And die a-moaning when your gut wound goes septic? Doesn't sound worth it to me." Sarah's arm didn't waver. "Time to leave. Now."

The drunk's mouth twisted as he weighed his chances. Jed couldn't stand it any longer.

"Son, she can put a bullet through each eye before you take another step, and that's if she's feeling generous. If she's at all cross, she'll shoot your balls off instead."

Sarah's aim shifted lower.

The drunk glanced at his crotch and made to cover it before catching himself and turning for the door. He stumbled out into the night.

When Jed turned back, the derringer was gone, and Sarah was giving him a cold stare. "I didn't need your help," she said. "He wouldn't have come any closer."

"I'm just trying to keep the peace and keep bloodstains off your floor."

Her head tilted for a moment before nodding. "Yes, I suppose you did save me from that horrible fate, Sheriff."

He put on his hat and touched the brim. "All in a day's work, ma'am."

Sarah's eyes crinkled with a smile. "Well, don't let me keep you from your duties."

Jed leaned on the bar, close enough to catch the lingering scent of soap from her afternoon bath. "Well that's just it. The way I see things, Mrs. Scott."

The doors flew open and the skinny form of Deputy Perkins burst through. "Sheriff Scott! The Six are in town!" The kid's eyes were round as full moons and looked all around the saloon as if more outlaws lurked the corners.

Jed's hands touched his pistols out of reflex as he headed for the door. His Sharps rifle was still racked in the office — would he have time to grab it? "Is it the bank?" he asked.

"No, there's one of 'em in your office, asking for you."

Jed stopped and placed a hand on the deputy's shoulder. "Just one, Sam?"

Perkins nodded.

"Alone? Which one?"

"Trigger Jones. Near fell through the door, chucked his gun belts on the floor, and demanded to see you, left his horse outside all in a lather."

"And you just left him there, alone with Otto?"

"Otto said he had it."

Normally, Jed would have been reassured. Otto Merrill was a good deputy, but he was as old as Sam was young and wasn't nearly up to the task of holding Trigger Jones. For all he knew, Otto could be dead already.

"I've got to go," he said to Sarah.

"Yes, you do. Be careful."

"Always am."

A blown Appaloosa snorted outside the jailhouse, too tired to pull at its lead. The old cavalryman within Jed felt his anger rise at the animal's mistreatment and promised himself to see the beautiful animal seen to before the night's end. He entered the jailhouse with his guns drawn, expecting a dead deputy on the floor and a ruckus over at the bank. Instead, he found Otto sitting in his chair, scattergun trained on a disarmed Trigger Jones, who looked like Satan himself had chased him across the plains.

The man's clothes were splattered with blood and coated in dust, and the skin on his hands were raw. The stench of blood, gunpowder, and stale sweat took Jed back to times he'd rather forget. It was the eyes that got him, though. On the few occasions Jed had set eyes on Trigger, the man had always looked like he was on the verge of telling a joke or stealing your woman. That man was gone, and in its place was a sorry soul who looked to Jed with a tired desperation.

"Sheriff," Trigger said, voice hoarse. He coughed. "I don't know how to say this."

"Save it," Jed said. He took Trigger's gun belt and hung it on a peg near his Sharps rifle, keeping an eye trained on the outlaw, just in case this was all an elaborate ruse. "Sam, go see to that Appaloosa outside."

"Appreciate it, Sheriff," Trigger said.

"You have until he gets back to explain yourself."

Trigger started, then stopped, then started again. A tale about stealing a coffin, and a monster inside it. What he described made no sense, a shadow that tore through half his crew like they were made of wet paper in a dozen heartbeats. "I need your help to go back and finish the thing off," Trigger said.

Jed nodded at the gun belt on the wall behind him. "You seem to have all the tools needed. What I'm curious about is why you didn't just run off into the hills on that mistreated animal of yours."

Cal shook his head in frustration, leaning back in his chair and letting his gaze drift over Jed's shoulder and stop at the old cavalry saber on the wall.

"You in the war?" Cal asked.

"I was. Mound's Battalion. Cavalry."

Cal hooked a thumb to his chest. "Scout for the Thirteenth Missouri. Reckon we were on opposite sides. I don't recollect if I ever took a shot at you. No hard feelings?"

Jed shrugged. "Bygones."

"One thing I learned in Hell was what I could run from and what I couldn't. Got to be a feeling that saved me in places where others made the wrong choice and got shot in the back. Likewise, I got to know what I could do with my squad and what we needed the rest of the company for.

"I don't know what this thing is, but I know if I run

from it, it'll catch me from behind, and I can't try taking it by myself and what's left of the Six. It's a job that'll need more guns."

"That's a fine tale, Trigger," Jed began.

"Don't like that name much, sheriff, Cal will do fine."

"All right, Cal. Look at it from where I'm standing. The leader of the Wild Six comes into my town, with tall tales of demon boxes, and expects me to just follow where he's leading. Where's the rest of your gang, Cal? Is there something waiting for me at the end of the trail, or are you scouting the town yourself right now?"

"You got kids, sheriff?" Cal asked.

"I do."

Cal tugged his shirt down, and pulled a rag bandage aside, revealing bloody furrows across his chest and shoulder. "This is what it did to me. It did worse to three of my men. You want it coming here and doing the same to your town, your kids? One of the coffin's carvings showed it eating babies and the like."

"What about your other men?"

Cal put his shirt back in place. "I'm here as a sign of good faith, Sheriff, but I'm not a total idiot. Pete and Bryan Carter are outside town waiting for me. I reckon they'll come around asking hard questions and taking matters into their own hands if I don't return tomorrow."

Jed looked to Otto, who seemed unsettled, but shrugged at Jed's unspoken question. He didn't believe all of Cal's story, either. The baby eating was obviously a lie, but something got the man rattled enough to walk into a jailhouse and hand over his guns.

It might be a trap, or some falling out among the gang that Trigger, or Cal, as he preferred, was maneuvering Jed into the middle of. It had all the earmarks of a trap. But those gouges on Cal's shoulder and chest were something else. They could have been made by an animal, he supposed, a bear or big cougar, but he suspected not. Cal had been facing his attacker, and he didn't believe there was any animal that could stand up to Cal's twin Navy .36s.

Jed couldn't figure out Cal's angle, if there was one, and as much as part of him suspected a trap, the other part sensed parts of the outlandish story were true, or at least that Cal believed it himself. Besides, after months chasing Cal and the rest of the Six, who were always melting into the hills before the posse caught up, this was a real chance to catch them on their back foot.

Jed holstered his gun and waved at Otto, who pointed the shotgun away from Cal's torso but wasn't keen to put it away entirely. "We'll head out in the morning," he said. "Those Williams boys going to be a problem?"

"Not if we're timely about it, and our truce holds."

"Truce?"

"You're gonna want us in on taking this monster down. In exchange, I want your word you'll give us a day's grace before we go back to our differences."

"What's to keep you from shooting me in the back?" Jed asked.

"You know I won't. My word means just as much as yours, Jedidiah."

Jed considered, then reached out. Cal took his hand and shook.

"You'll need more men," Cal said, giving a glance to Otto.

"I'll fetch up a posse."

Cal winced but nodded.

"You need a doctor for that?" Jed said, nodding at Cal's bandage.

"Nah, I've had worse. Could stand to take a load off though."

"You can bunk here," Jed said.

"You tossing me in a cell?"

"Something like that. Your guns, I'm locking up. The cell will stay open."

Sam came in, taking in the lack of pointed guns. "Horse is at the livery getting seen to. Reverend Graham caught me and said there's been a landslide at the pass. Trail's completely blocked unless you fancy climbing over it yourself or riding a mountain goat. We're not gonna get any more wagon traffic in until it's cleared. Also looks like someone shot up a bunch of Dust Crows."

Jed looked to Cal. "Your doing?"

Cal spread his hands. "They tried bushwhacking us for the coffin as we came into the valley. Found out they weren't up to the task." He paused, then scratched at his stubble. "Someone in the fray started playing with dynamite and brought down the hillside."

"You see who did it?"

Cal shook his head. "You know how confusing a gunfight is, Sheriff. It was dark besides."

Jed shook his head and turned back to Sam. "Right. I'll send a wire to the territorial office for a work gang. If the railroad sees fit to finish the bridge over Chorizo Gorge on time, we won't have to bring supplies through on mules."

"But what if they're late?" Otto said.

"We've got enough here to tide us for another month at least, maybe two, and that's not counting what the ranches have. My brother's place is probably set until fall." He poked Otto's pot belly. "Don't worry, Deputy Merrill, you won't die of starvation."

Sam fidgeted and kept looking to the street. "Anything else, Sam?"

"That fella Mrs. Scott almost shot passed out, so I drug him into the street and rolled him in the back of the wagon he showed up in. The damn fool has a crate of sweating nitro back there, and I don't know what to do."

Jed's gaze shot across the street to a wagon and tiny wood box filled with straw marked NITROGLYCERIN. Cal took a breath to get himself under control, but Otto was already moving.

"Don't worry about it, Sheriff. I'll put it somewhere safe. Fucking cowboys."

"That old coot not afraid of it exploding?" Cal asked as they watched Otto gently lift the box, talking to it like a scared animal and walking away.

"Otto's nothing if not steady," Jed said. "Come on."

He got Cal situated in a cell and left the barred door ajar. Jed watched Cal lay back on the bunk's thin pad and fall asleep instantly. The bandit's guns were safely locked up with Sam and Otto trading off on watching the cell block, guns in hand. If it was true the Six and the Crows had thinned each other out a bit, perhaps it explained what brought on Cal's gambit. If anything, Jed was more keen to see the situation for himself, though he figured he'd need more men for the posse.

He thought over Cal's story one more time, wondering what the heat had done to the man to come up with such a tale. Stone coffins, smoke monsters, Latin inscriptions… He made a mental note to ask the Reverend Graham to come along to help translate. And besides, if there was even a kernel of truth to Cal's tall tale, it wouldn't hurt to have the Lord on their side. That, and a well-armed militia.

Chapter Twelve

THE CELLBLOCK WAS DARK APART FROM A PALE MOONBEAM across the brickwork. Cal thought the deputies would stay up all night, keeping a shotgun leveled in case he should try charging through the open door, but the deputy's empty chair just outside the cell was empty. Something had woken Cal up, his sleeping self warning of grave danger without details. It was too late to run away. He had forgotten something, or left it unfinished, and it was coming for him. He stood and crossed to the cell door, discovering it closed and locked. The lamps in the sheriff's office were dark, too. Jedidiah Scott hadn't trusted him after all and had broken his word. Cal raised his fist to pound on the door when something scraped behind him.

Red eyes glowed from the corner. Cal tried turning away, but his limbs were like concrete and refused to move even as his heart thumped like it was trying to burst through his ribs. The creature whispered, but the words made no sense to him, teasing at him in a language he had forgotten, one he could remember if his chest didn't explode first.

It wanted him.

Whispers of power.

Calvin Jones, prince of the night with an empire of servants, second only to a master who outshone the sun.

In the cell, an oily hand reached for his heart, taloned fingertips sinking into him, flesh parting like soft butter. His ribs creaked as the fingers wiggled past. The pain!

Cal woke up to a startled deputy, his chair overturned and looking over a shotgun barrel aimed right at Cal's thumping heart. Cal's face dripped, shirt plastered to him with sweat and turning chill. His ears stung with the ghost of a scream, half-remembered. His own? His cell door was open, as promised, with sunlight streaming through the barred window.

Cal let out a breath and smiled as he raised his hands. "Easy, deputy. Just had a dream that I was in jail. Imagine my surprise."

The fat deputy, Otto, lowered the gun slightly. "Sheriff will be around presently."

Cal sat back on the bunk and leaned against the warming brick wall. "I expect he will."

THEY FED him and put him on his own horse before all six feet of Sheriff Scott arrived and slapped a set of manacles around his wrists.

"That's hardly neighborly," Cal said. "The Williams boys might mistake the sight of me in irons as threatening."

Jed patted Rocky's neck and handed Cal the reins. "Stayed up a bit late last night and took a ride outside town. Found the remains of a campfire around Crested

Butte and a fresh set of prints leading back into the hills. That is where you left Pete and Bryan, isn't it?"

Cal had gambled on Pete following orders and lost. He kept a smile on his face and swallowed his anger. "Might be they were being careful. Pete and Bryan perhaps thought something went wrong and they needed to find a better vantage point when the sheriff came riding outta town without me."

Jed fixed Cal with a pale-eyed stare. "Might be. Or maybe they decided to run back to your hideout and warn the others we're coming."

"There are no others," Cal said. "None that are alive anyway."

Jed went to his horse, a beautiful chestnut with a white blaze, cinched his saddlebags, and checked the action on his repeater before sliding it into a case. "We'll discover that together, won't we?"

They headed off, a half-dozen in all. Jed left the fat deputy in charge of the town and brought along the kid, Sam, all knees and elbows trying to look tough in the saddle. Beside him rode a thin-haired man on a mule, a reverend of some sort named Graham who didn't mind getting made whenever he looked askance at Cal. Sunset's mayor, Hornsby, rode ahead of him with the sheriff, dressed like a dandy and wearing pistol that seemed a little heavy for his hip. It diminished Cal's opinion of the towns-folk that a man as buck-toothed as Hornsby could get their votes. Or maybe it was just that no one else wanted the job.

Taking the rear was an out-of-work ranch hand called Porter, a beefy fella Cal had fought once, drunk. He didn't remember who had won, but from the flat looks he was getting, Porter might be spoiling for a rematch. Come to think of it, Porter owed him money, too.

Cal guided them through the trails, wondering what happened to Pete and Bryan. He hoped that they didn't get it in their heads to try to rescue him, not that that was something to come naturally to Pete or Bryan. They would rather shoot their way out of the situation rather than try talking first. But as they went along, even Cal could pick out the two sets of prints, no more than a few hours old, that had to have been Pete and Bryan heading straight back to the ranch. Cal probably could have caught up to them on Rocky, but the reverend's mule couldn't muster more than a plod. Doubtless the animal could go for days and days without complaint, but speedy it was not.

The sun tipped near noon when they got to the ranch, and the sheriff called a halt short of the collapsed-out buildings for a look around. Fresh boot prints trampled all over the place, with Byron's especially noticeable on account of his new boots. The other set of prints were likely his brother's, but there was a third that was an odd mix between a man's foot and some kind of beast, with deep pads and sharp claws that sent an ache through Cal's bandaged shoulder.

"Looks like your boys have flown the coop," Jed said.

"I can't say I'm not surprised, Sheriff, but I hoped that they would have at least shown me some more loyalty. On the other hand, it doesn't look like there's anyone else around. Man 'nor beast," Cal said, mouth working as he puzzled out the strange footprints in the dust.

Cal led them to the barn and held out the manacles. "Mind setting these loose? If that monster is still in there, I'd rather face it with half a chance."

Jed's gaze went to the darkened barn for a moment, then the strange footprints in the dust, before nodding and unlocking the manacles. "Don't expect me to give you a gun."

He shrugged and cursed the Williams brothers in his head. "Fair enough."

"And you're going in first," Jed said, his pale-eyed stare daring him to say otherwise.

Cal held the sheriff's gaze, just to see how long until the man blinked. When Cal realized the other man would wait until doomsday, he nodded and stepped to the barn.

The door was still open.

He paused before going inside. Sun beams lanced through shadow, dust motes sparkling as they fell. The air was heavy, stagnant, with an undercurrent of blood. The coffin was ajar with its lid off to the side. Cal took a step closer, fists clenching and unclenching, wondering if he'd get clawed from the front by the monster or shot in the back from the posse's crossfire. He let out a breath an took another step before peering into the sarcophagus.

Empty. No body, no dust, no nothing. To the right and left, on the barn floor, were bits and pieces of Silas, Rubin, and Ben, all gathered up in a macabre jigsaw version of each man. Their remains were all withered, wrinkled skin dry as fallen leaves, looking more like dolls made of crepe paper than flesh. Someone behind him swore, then excused themselves in front of the reverend.

The Reverend Graham himself came forward to Cal's side and rested a hand on his shoulder before kneeling down by each man, murmuring blessings under his breath, palm out, not quite touching the men but making signs of the cross over their remains.

"May the Lord guide their souls to peace," Reverend Graham said.

Paper skin curled and fluttered in the breeze, peeling away in ribbons. Cal pressed a hand to his bandaged shoulder. "Damned near got me, too," he said.

"You're a lucky man, then."

Cal didn't know what to say to that, so he walked away. The posse fanned out and searched the farm, finding nothing. Cal overheard the kid, Sam, talking to Jed.

"I thought there'd be more," Sam said, wiping his mouth.

"More what?" Jed asked.

"More loot, I guess. Or a fancy hideout dug into a cave with money, gold, rings and such heaped in piles. These men live more like dogs."

Cal scuffed his boot in the dirt, and Sam flinched. His eyes widened as he met Cal's look and his mouth opened with some apology, but Cal didn't bother listening as he decided he'd needed to find some sun. Porter held a rifle in white-knuckled hands and raised the barrel. Cal got the message and settled for leaning against the barn door just at the shadow's edge.

Reverend Graham bent over the Latin inscriptions, a dirt-smudged finger dragging under each word as he read. His eyes had that same cast revivalist preachers had at tent shows, brimstone smoldering under thick eyebrows at some affront to his piety.

"There was only one of us that could read it, and not well," Cal said. "Can you make heads or tails of it?"

Graham wiped his mouth with the back of his wrist. "My seminarian semester of Latin predates the secession, but my recall is mustering. These are the remains of one Lord Braga, the last of his line."

"We got the name, and all saw the scenes carved into the sides. Are those scenes true, or just some madman's fancy?"

Graham narrowed his eyes as he walked around the sarcophagus, tapping a finger to his lips, he circled twice before turning to Cal. "Mister Jones," Reverend Graham began.

"Just Cal, reverend."

"Mister Cal, what you and your men found were the remains of a cursed soul. Braga was the leader of a holy order of knights. Hardened men of several campaigns in what's now Prussia, if I'm not mistaken." He pointed at the carvings on the outer sarcophagus. "Braga was a rich and pious man, laid to rest with honor for his service to the church."

Cal sensed the reverend's hesitation. "But?"

Graham's lips pressed into a bloodless line. "I believe this outer sarcophagus was commissioned long after Braga's death. The inner coffin tells a more disturbing story than its crude pictures convey. Braga died from his quest to rid the land of a monster that laid waste to a whole garrison in a newly conquered province."

Deputy Sam pointed. "That's them, forcing the monster into the coffin?"

"No, Braga *is* the monster. Whoever inscribed this, he wanted it made plain Braga was sent to his certain death against the monster by his order's abbot, who wanted Braga out of the way. Except Braga survived the encounter with grievous wounds. Days later, Braga recovered and slaughtered all within the monastery, draining them of all their blood. His remaining brothers in arms chased after him, then defeated him at great cost. Braga's minions were beheaded or burned on pyres, but Braga was left with a stake driven through his heart and sealed in the casket out of respect for the man he was."

"We found the stake, a length of wood about the size of my forearm, capped in gold. Braga's body was all sallow until we removed it, that's when it — he — woke up."

"The beast has unnatural healing powers, fueled by feeding on the lifeblood of its victims."

Cal felt sick. "Our bullets slowed it some, but it seemed no more bothered than being stung by a bee."

"Where is the stake now?" Jed asked.

"We left it on the floor, I would have thought. I guess Pete and Bryan took it with them. What I don't get is how this Braga didn't kill them."

"Perhaps Braga needed allies more than victims. The text suggests he could turn men into creatures like himself."

Sam's face paled. "Who would agree to that?"

Cal thought back to his dream that morning. "Pete always would go with the best offer. Can I bury my men? I owe 'em that."

Jed's grimace softened when Graham laid a hand on the sheriff's shoulder. "It's the Christian thing to do, Jed."

"If you say so, Reverend, but make it quick." Jed turned and went to see to his horse.

THE OTHERS BROUGHT the remains of Silas, Ben, and Rubin into the sunlight, feather-light like broken piñatas. In fact, Cal wouldn't have been able to tell one from the other apart from their clothing and hair color. It made it easier for Cal to imagine these were not the men he knew, just effigies for their missing bodies. He clung to that and ignored the voice in his head scratching the inside of his skull like a caged wildcat, reliving the attack and imagining Braga's dark form *feeding* from each man, gurgling as the last drops of their blood were sucked dry.

Reverend Graham ended the brief service, and when he made the sign of the cross, the bodies started smoking without flames, while also sending Cal's chest and shoulder tingling. The men jumped back, but within seconds, the bodies were nothing but ash outlines of jigsaw men and empty clothes.

Cal was the first to recover. "Dust to dust."

There came a great crack like a gunshot from the barn. More smoke rose through the roof. They rushed in, guns drawn, to find the sarcophagus and coffin split and in pieces. The black film on the coffin's inside turned to ash. Without knowing why, Cal reached out and brushed the ash away, revealing more Latin.

"Reverend?"

Graham pushed his way through the spooked men and ran a finger under the letters. "If thou would fight this beast, this … this… The word's not Latin. Wam-pyr? Vampire? … Arm thyself with stakes of wood or silver and impale their hearts. Sharpen thy blades and remove heads from bodies. Speak the blessings of the Lord to purge their damned souls. And when all else should fail, force thy foe into the sun's cleansing fire.

"It seems not everyone associated with Lord Braga's internment was convinced he'd stay dead," Graham said.

"What do we do now, Sheriff?" asked Hornsby. "Even if we take all this Latin poppycock at face value, which I remain unconvinced, this so-called Lord Braga and the Williams brothers could be a threat to the citizenry."

Graham nodded at the coffin. "The inscriptions don't specify the number, but it took a small army to take down Braga in his lair."

"They obviously found a way with wooden stakes and swords back then," Hornsby said. "We ought to do at least as well, or improve on their methods in these modern times."

"We're going to need more men if he digs in somewhere," Porter said.

Jed took a glance at the sky and grunted. "Then let's

mount up while the sun's still shining." He tilted his head at Cal, thinking for a moment before seemingly coming to a decision. He pulled a pistol from the left side of his gun rig and handed it over. "You might need this."

Cal took the gun, a government-issue Starr not unfamiliar to his hand. It was serviceable, though not his style. He tucked the gun into his belt. "That's mighty trusting of you, Sheriff. You're not afraid I'll shoot you with your own gun?"

Jed was already mounting his horse. "Just don't make me regret it."

Chapter Thirteen

JUST BECAUSE JED DECIDED HE COULD TRUST CAL JONES with a gun didn't mean he would ride with his back to the man. The outlaw and his spotted Appaloosa rode point as they followed those damned strange footprints running down the center of the trail, bold as you like. By early afternoon, Jed reckoned they'd reached their destination on account of a cloud of buzzards circling over the hoodoos on oily wings.

The abandoned mining camp was an even more sorry sight than the Six's ranch. Jed wished the wind would turn and take the buzzing flies and growing stench away. It reminded him too much of the trenches and bulwarks surrounding Vicksburg around the time the surrounded populace had turned to eating their own horses and, as rumor had it, each other.

The shack before him was a hodgepodge of wood scavenged from crates, rail tie scraps, and local scrub held together with nails, rope, and bits of wire. A spotty coat of creosote made it look half-burnt, and perhaps part of it was, for all Jed knew. Barely big enough for a man to curl up in and enough holes in the walls that'd just annoy a raindrop, it seemed to Jed that the man who built it was unnaturally optimistic, or maybe one of the lazy types that gave up once things edged past easy. Not that it mattered now. The Dust Crow within it stared back at him with clouded eyes and a half-smile courtesy of his missing throat and jawbone. Not that different from Vicksburg at all, he thought.

Bodies of Dust Crows littered the camp, riddled with bullet holes and slashed to ribbons. He watched Cal Jones walking among them, setting his feet in the footprints in the dirt, stutter-stepping and leaping as he tried, and failed, following along. Reverend Graham sat on his mule with his head lowered and quoting scripture to himself. Sam and the rest of the posse gathered upwind of the slaughter, and Jed couldn't bring himself to blame them.

Cal brushed dirt from his pants and knocked the dust off his black hat. "What do you reckon?" Jed asked.

"It don't make sense. It's just Pete and Bryan that did this," Cal said.

"Not that monster, Braga?"

"Naw, he just stood over there, far as I can tell." Cal pointed to the camp's lone tree.

"So the Williams boys shot up six Crows, and Braga came by after?"

Cal shook his head. "Braga never set foot inside the camp itself. This was all Pete and Bryan, but it's not their style at all. Bryan favors his Bowie, but these slashes aren't clean." He fingers brushed absently at his bandaged shoulder. "Pete likes to pick his marks off at a distance, but he was in the thick of it. They just ran in the middle of camp and started shooting. No ambush, no shooting from cover, no sneaking up with a knife. And no Bowie or pistol rips throats and jawbones out. They would have been in crossfire, Pete and Bryan, but it didn't matter. I couldn't even follow some of their moves, 'less I had wings. They moved like wolves and jumped like antelope."

"Braga has recruited them to his cause," Reverend Graham said. "Minions and henchmen, the carvings said, recruited from the fallen and the wicked."

Cal took stock of the camp, counted the bodies. "Then we might have a larger problem," he said. "I'd say there were a dozen Crows camped here, give or take, but there are only six bodies."

"Maybe they turned tail. Wouldn't be the first time," Jed said.

"Might done," Cal allowed, "but if the Reverend has it right, Braga might have been recruiting."

Sam walked into the camp, keeping his eyes fixed on Jed and tiptoeing around the bodies. He felt for the kid, he had once been that kid, until he'd learned how to get used to mangled flesh. Jed would have to noodle on how best to caution Sam about the dreams he'd be soon having without giving him the notion Jed was calling him a coward. That was almost as dangerous as pulling a gun on a man, sometimes.

Sam waved him over. "Picked up another set of tracks. The ones we followed from the ranch went south on foot. Then there's another set, mounted. Looked to be heading for the trail back to Sunset."

"How many?"

"Three, maybe more," Sam said.

"We should keep on with Braga and the Williams," Cal said.

"If the Reverend is right, we should go back to town," Sam said. "Otto ain't up to holding off the Crows by himself."

"We let Braga go, there's no telling what he'll do to those out in the valley away from town," Cal said.

"How we know it's not just some rabid cougar done all this?" asked Mayor Hornsby, dismounting.

"Are you serious, man? You already forget what we saw this morning?" Cal said.

Hornsby put a finger in Cal's face. "I know I have not seen monsters eating babies, that's for sure. Dead bodies and a tragedy, had they been God-fearing men, but I have also been to many a carnival show where hucksters and illusionists use gunpowder, trained animals, and chemicals to affect illusions and prey on the weak-minded. Well I, sir, stand forearmed and forewarned."

Cal batted the finger away. "You're calling all this a snake oil show?"

"Whose story has this been all along? Yours, Trigger Jones. Yours."

"The name's Cal."

Hornsby spread his hands and pursed his lips. "Your wanted poster says different. If I were in your shoes, Trigger, I might think to pull a fast one on us, using an animal attack and carnival tricks to draw out the law while the rest of the gang circles back into town while Sheriff Scott's away."

Cal's fingers twitched closer to the gun tucked in his belt, and Jed made ready for drawing his own. Hornsby didn't seem to notice. "You're a damned fool, Mayor," Cal said after a moment. "Tell him, Sheriff."

Jed stepped between the two and crouched for a closer look at a dead Crow. Could it have been an animal? Sure. If it had been one body mauled in the armed camp and not six.

Jed squinted and looked back towards Sunset, picturing the Crows storming into town, Otto hobbling down the street on his busted leg and getting cut down from behind. Sarah might hold out in the saloon for a while, but the rest of town was mostly softer folk. Folk he had an obligation to, their women and children also. Hornsby was a pig-headed jackass, sure, but that didn't make him wrong. Jed had to consider the possibility he'd been suckered.

"It seems to me," he began, and his words dried up. Acrid smoke seared his nostrils, making his eyes water. When he blinked the tears away, he turned to find Reverend Graham with his hand on a dead man's fore-head, praying for the man's soul as smoke billowed out of two holes puncturing the Crow's neck.

"Is the Reverend in on it, too, Mayor?" Cal said. "He playing carnival tricks, is he?

Hornsby fumed and sputtered. "We don't know how long these men have been here. This could all be coinci-dence, or some magician's trick you've yet to reveal."

"If I were, I sure wouldn't be wasting my talents out here," Cal said.

Graham finished with the man and moved onto the next body, which began smoking from its neck as Graham started his prayer.

"You were saying, Sheriff?" Cal said.

Cal Jones might be many things, but a magician he was not. As to what killed the Crows, it was plain to him that the Williams brothers and this Braga character, human or not, was the greater threat, and those tracks led deeper into the valley and its isolated farmsteads. If those tracks kept their general heading... His stomach dropped and he made his decision. "We'll follow the men who went off on foot," he said, walking over and setting a foot into a stirrup.

"Sheriff! What about Sunset? I demand we head back and defend the town," Hornsby said.

Jed spit the dust from his mouth. "Mayor, your concern

may be for the town, and that's your own business. But I'm the sheriff of not just Sunset, but the entire valley. Homesteader's got just as much right to my protection as a shopkeeper." He hauled himself into the saddle, touching heels to Cactus before Hornsby could respond.

Hornsby could cause him a heap of trouble if he was wrong, but his gut told him this was the right call. Besides, between the earlier damage the Wild Six had done, and this attack on the camp, there couldn't be more than a handful of Crows left.

Chapter Fourteen

THE OTHERS WERE ON EDGE, AND CAL RECKONED IT WAS about damn time. A few hours past the Crow massacre gave the posse time to catch up on the nightmare, minds shaking off their excuses and wiping the bullshit from their eyes as their bowels turned watery. The posse rode stiff-backed and tight-shouldered, like as not to tire themselves out in the next hour if they weren't careful. Of course if the monster Braga, this vampire, as Reverend Graham called him, caught up to them in the dark, stiff backs wouldn't figure into it at all.

Cal heard his name and looked up. The sheriff's glare was a hair from requiring a tussle, but Cal swallowed the urge, for now. "You're lagging. Keep up," Jed said.

Cal glanced back at the reverend on his mule behind him, and the baby-faced deputy bringing up the rear. "I ain't the hindmost, sheriff," he said. "Besides, we go any faster, we're liable to miss a track or head down a false trail."

Jed hooked a thumb at the men. "I don't expect

Graham's mule to keep pace, and Sam is there to watch the back trail." He poked a finger at Cal's chest. "I want you to stay with Hornsby, got it?"

Normally this is where Cal would start tussling. But he felt the eyes of the others on him and sensed how little it would take for someone to pull on him. Instead, he eased his horse away from Jed's and clicked his tongue. Rocky picked up his feet and they caught up to Hornsby. Jed thundered past them, back up the trail and shouting to Porter.

Hornsby's shoulders hunched over in the saddle, eyes on the ground rather than searching the jagged ridges above and blackened escarpments closing in beside them. The man was like as ready to bolt at a moment's notice, should anything rise up from the hip-high weeds and attack.

"Sheriff seems to like a tight ship," Cal said.

The mayor startled but recovered quickly. "A sight more discipline than you're used to, I'd wager," Hornsby said.

"You'd be surprised," Cal said. "But that's beside the point. You're all riding spooked."

"And you're not?"

"I swallowed it."

"That's a good idea, Trigger Jones. Take that idea a bit further and swallow your lip, too. I don't have time for it." He said it offhand, distracted. The mayor's eyes were fixed ahead, not really seeing anything.

Cal gripped the reigns tighter and felt Rocky gathering under him, reading his tension. He ran a hand along the horse's neck to soothe it, as much as himself. Rising to Hornsby's bait wouldn't help him none, might even get him back in irons.

Jed shouted at Porter and turned back to wave the rest of them along.

Cal let Rocky trot ahead and he nodded at a pile of bleached deer bones to Hornsby's left. "Pick up your gait, Mayor, you're liable to get left behind. Ain't no one gonna vote for you if you're dead."

THE SUN DIPPED LOWER in the sky, dropping the heat a notch below baking. Cal tipped the last of his canteen's water, alkaline and bitter, leaving his mouth all soapy-like, but better than parched. Reverend Graham and Deputy Perkins were dots on the ridge behind them. Cal kept checking over his shoulder, expecting them to disappear or get cut down by an ambush. It's what he would have done if he saw the group split like this. Let the lead horses through, then circle back, and devil take the hindmost. If anything, Jed had sped them up, spoken orders shortening to single grunted syllables, and riding back and forth along the trail. The horses needed to rest a spell, but Jed kept them going. Rocky labored beneath Cal, and he thought about pulling to the side regardless, girding himself for a tongue-lashing from the irritable posse.

"Almost there, Rocky," he said.

They crested a rise that overlooked a ranch next to a trickling stream. Cal hoped its water tasted sweeter than what was in his canteen. The ranch itself looked prosperous enough, which in Sunset Valley meant it still had cattle and unwithered crops. Granted, the cows were thin and lethargic, laying down under the trees along the stream's edge, and the fields had a yellow tinge to them that could have been caused by some blight he hadn't yet heard of.

Jed shouted and kicked his horse in a full gallop. Porter was only a beat behind him, giving his mount the spurs. Hornsby swore and put his heels to his horse's flanks, waving at Cal to hurry along. Cal murmured an apology to Rocky before sending him into a gallop.

"What gives?" Cal shouted at Hornsby's back.

"This's John's ranch."

"John who?"

"Scott. Jed's brother."

"I don't see—" Cal began, but then he picked out what Jed must have. A body face-down in the corral, and he realized the cattle weren't resting, not with tongues lolling in the dust and dark eyes clouding over.

Cal shook off his surprise and took another quick look around. He didn't like it. The trail's dust must have clogged his brains, because when he surveyed at the farm with an outlaw's eye, he saw a job gone bad. Or job about to.

He set fingers to his mouth and sent out a shrieking whistle. Hornsby and Porter's heads turned, but the sheriff thundered on.

"Ambush!" he called out.

Hornsby hesitated but Porter said something and the two turned to chase after Sheriff Scott. Cal swore and rode after them, expecting gunfire from the buildings on their flank. When it didn't come, he decided their trap lay in the barn or the house. Something waiting for them to dismount and barge in, where the posse's advantage in speed and guns would evaporate.

The fools charged forward anyway. What did that make him for following? He should turn aside now and ride halfway across the valley before darkness fell. Take his chances with the blocked trail and then onto San Francisco come morning.

Whoever had lived here was already dead. The sheriff

had to know that, brother or not. A man had to ignore that spark of hope sometimes. That hope would get you killed.

But if it had been Jenny? He'd have chased that spark to the end.

He patted Jenny's cross in his pocket. He'd see this through, then leave. The greater fool, he.

Chapter Fifteen

THE OTHERS HAD PULLED UP SHORT OF THE HOUSE AND dismounted with guns drawn. Cal tied off Rocky with the other horses, not trusting the animal to stay put with the air reeking of blood.

"John! It's Jedidiah!" the sheriff called out.

Porter and Hornsby shouted as well, cupping hands to mouths.

Nothing.

Cal pitched his voice quiet, so only Jed could hear. "I don't like this, Sheriff. It feels like a trap."

The sheriff turned towards Cal, but his eyes weren't seeing him. Cal reached for his shoulder, but Jed shrugged him off and headed for the house. Something knocked inside it, followed by a squeak. Jed broke into a run.

Time stretched as Cal ran after Jed. He felt eyes on him. The wounds at his shoulder twinged. His eyes went to the darkened windows, looking for the glint of a gun barrel, a shadow against a shadow, a pair of red eyes in the darkness. The gun in his hand felt off, the Starr's balance just a smidge too forward. His aim would be just that much lower than his Navy, and he only had the six shots, the sheriff not having given him any reloads.

This was dumb. He should have run away.

He ran into Jed, who stopped just inside the doorway.

Cal dropped to a knee and swept the room, too slow! He twisted around to get the fucker with the knife hiding behind the door — nothing.

Time sped up, back to normal. With it, his brain caught up with what his senses had filtered out.

The entry hall was a charnel house. Two men lay with their heads at unnatural angles, faces painted red with their own blood, throats torn open, exposing ragged windpipes and glistening spines. In the sitting room beyond, a woman's arm clutched a fireplace poker five feet from where the rest of her body lay in a bloody heap. The walls were gouged and puckered with bullet holes, as was the ceiling.

Jed was on his knees, shaking the body of one of the dead men. "John," he repeated, almost a whisper, and Cal wondered if the sheriff knew he was making the sound.

Footsteps thudded on the porch. Cal whirled in time to see Porter and Hornsby take in the scene and then disappear, both retching. Cal turned back, sensing the gorge within him rising, but not so much he couldn't force it back down.

He crouched near the sheriff and kept an eye on the hallway and darkened staircase. "How many lived here, Sheriff?" When the man didn't respond, he tried again. "Jed, John's gone. Look at me."

Jed turned to Cal, still staring through him, then over his shoulder to the woman in the parlor.

"Jed, how many? Who still might be alive?"

"John, Caroline, Molly, plus three hands."

"Okay." Cal counted on fingers, then folded back a

digit for each body in the house and the one out in the corral. Porter and Hornsby returned, still looking green. With the sheriff still in shock, it was up to him to keep the others focused on himself and not the bodies.

"There's two left that might be holed up. We're going to go through the house. I'll go first, and if I get shot in the back, I'll be right pissed. Got it?"

The two nodded and Cal figured it was the best he could do for now.

The kitchen held nothing more than the fixings for supper scattered across the floor and a dented coffee pot in the corner. Cal hadn't expected to find anything there anyway. Anyone alive would have come running when they entered the house, and there wasn't enough cover for a proper bushwhack, unlike the upstairs. With the lower floor cleared, Cal stepped over the carnage and readied himself at the landing.

The shadows clung thick to the top of the staircase. Cal put his back to the wall and kept his gun trained on the darkest shadow. The boards creaked under his boots, and he ducked his head under a low beam. A smashed chair came into view as he approached the top step, splinters and stuffing embedded in the upper floor's pine slats. Blood streaked along the wall, leading to the farthest of three bedrooms.

Cal poked his head into the first open doorway, a small, cramped room with a rag doll lying on the floor next to a small dresser with a cloudy mirror. Cal used the mirror to study the room's blind corners, clear enough for him to tell there were no bodies and no surprises waiting for them.

He motioned the others to follow down the hall. He twisted the next room's door handle slow and let the door creak open. He crouched low, half expecting a shotgun blast to tear through the door and cut him in half, if he were stupid enough to stand in front of it, or try barreling his way through. He waited as the door *creak-creak-creaked* loud in everyone's ears. He gathered himself and poked his head around the door at knee-level.

The dead man stared back at him, eyes rolled to the whites, close enough that Cal spotted a patch of scruff the man had missed shaving from his chin that morning. A checked shirt, dungarees, and limp fingers curled around a shotgun. The rest of the room held nothing more than a small desk, and low bed, pristine covers neatly folded and ready for a night's rest.

The dead man had been drained of blood, but not in that sunken way Cal's men had, more like the dead Crows. Two punctures at his leathery, bruised throat were all that marked him.

"Toby Burnside," Jed muttered. "Top hand."

Cal took the shotgun and broke open the breach. Still loaded.

Cal handed the shotgun back to Porter and motioned at the third doorway with the bloodstain leading to it. He waved the others to the sides, and checked on Jed, who still seemed shook, but was snapping out of it. Cal raised both eyebrows in question and Jed nodded. As good as it was going to get. Cal touched the calico in his pocket for luck and tried the handle. He pushed the door open, counted to two, and fell to his shoulder across the threshold, gun swinging up.

The room was filled with furniture and steamer trunks, some things a sight finer than one would expect in a farmer's house, all piled into a corner that couldn't have hid a man or monster unless they were skinny as a rattler. Cal pushed himself up, gun trained on the pile nonetheless.

A flicker of movement.

Cal shifted his aim.

The pile shuddered.

Cal fired, as Jed hit him from the side, sending the shot high. Cal swung the pistol around and had it knocked from his hand as a blur hit Jed full in the chest, sending him tumbling. Cal scrambled for the gun, fingertips singing on the hot barrel, re-gripping, swinging on target when Mayor Hornsby stepped in front of him, hands out.

"Woah, woah, woah! It's a kid, Trigger!" Hornsby said.

Cal checked his fire and looked past the mayor. A skinny girl with dark curls had her arms clamped around Jed's shoulders, head buried in the sheriff's chest.

"It's all right, Molly. Uncle Jed's got you," Jed said. He patted her head, and clarity returned to his eyes.

Cal's back itched. The room felt all wrong, and he had the sudden inclination to get the hell out of the house.

"Time to leave, gents," he said. The others must have felt it, too, as they shied away from the walls and long shadows the setting sun cast through the window.

The home creaked. Porter turned and cried out, swinging the shotgun around. The gun boomed in the tiny space, and something fell on Porter from the ceiling before ravaging his neck and pulling the man into the doorway.

Cal couldn't get a clear shot, but that didn't stop Hornsby from firing. Two rounds blew through Porter's back, another went wide and splintered the door jamb. A part of Cal noted the girl, Molly, screaming and Jed putting himself between her and the danger, backing them towards the room's window.

Porter fell limp to the floor, and his attacker smiled at Cal.

"Hello, bossman," Bryan said. Porter's blood smeared his lips and slid off gleaming canines. His brown eyes had glowing red flakes in them.

Bryan flung himself at Cal.

Cal dropped and put a heel into the man's belly as he passed overhead.

Bryan's talons caught his boot heel and spun him around. Cal's head snapped back, and bright light flashed as his skull cracked against the floor.

Keep moving!

Wind on his face as someone passed him by.

More gunshots.

Cal got to his feet, where Jed and Hornsby dangled from Bryan's outstretched arms even as they unloaded their pistols into his body. Bryan flinched and grunted under the impacts, his blood-smeared face contorting in pain, but not going down. Cal fired his last, and Bryan's head snapped as the bullet took him between the eyes.

Jed and Hornsby stumbled to the floor as Bryan's hands went slack. Bryan wavered, and for a moment, Cal thought that was the end of it. Instead, Bryan righted himself, and the bullet in his brain pushed itself through the closing hole in his skull before thudding to the floor.

"That'll cost you, Trigger," Bryan growled.

Bryan fell on him. Cal and Bryan had tussled and wrestled a few times over the years, and while Bryan had the edge in strength, Cal had always more than held his own with speed, leverage, and self-tutelage from getting knocked down in countless brawls. He always had Bryan's measure, and it was never a real contest between them.

Red-eyed Bryan was different. His strength had multiplied, and his hands were rattlesnake-quick, countering every hand break and counter Cal threw at him. Bryan leaned in, jaws snapping at his neck, the stench of blood with an undercurrent of corruption gagging Cal.

"You picked wrong, Cal," Bryan whispered. "Lord

Braga never forgets a slight. Be glad it's me and not him or Pete that ends you."

Something rocked them both. Bryan's weight came off as Jed put a forearm across Bryan's neck and levered the vampire's head back. Bryan's hold slipped, and Cal twisted away. The three tumbled across a sunbeam. Flesh sizzled and inhuman strength smashed Cal and Jed together as Bryan tried pulling free.

"Window," Jed grunted.

The two scrambled, one each on Bryan's arms. Bryan hissed and surged back. Boots slid across the wood floor.

Hornsby crawled on hands and knees and snatched up the shotgun. Bryan lunged at Cal, slipping free from Jed's grip. Canines sunk into Cal's wounded shoulder, though only the tips penetrated the bandages. It was enough to re-open the wounds and Cal felt numbness crawl across his body and his strength fading. The voice of his jail cell nightmare whispered in his head.

Join me, and all will be forgiven.

A shotgun boomed, and Bryan fell back, his left knee shattered. The voice faded as Cal's strength returned. He wasted no time, joining Jed in picking Bryan up and running headlong to the window.

Bryan's flesh smoked as they approached, then caught fire as his body broke through glass. Talons gouged and sank into the window frame. Bryan, now fully engulfed in writhing flame, pulled himself up to the sill, then went flying backwards as Jed's boot caught him square in the chest.

Bryan the fireball landed in the yard, thrashing with broken limbs and flesh sizzling like bacon. In moments, the movements stopped and the flames died, leaving behind a vaguely man- shaped pile of ashes and acrid smoke.

There will be no escape, the voice said as it faded entirely. Cal hung his head out the window and retched.

Chapter Sixteen

THE AIR SMELT OF IRON AND BURNT, ROTTEN FLESH, TAKING Jed back to battlefields he'd purposely forgotten. He screwed his eyes tight and cleared the stench with a powerful exhale, then pulled a bandanna over his nose before his next breath. It didn't help the smell much, but did keep the memories at bay.

Jed left Molly with Reverend Graham while he headed back into the house to see to his brother's remains. Cal, Sam, and Hornsby had placed the bodies in the hallway, wrapped in bedclothes for shrouds. Jed could just about figure out who lay under each sheet, but peeled back his brother's out of some notion he wouldn't sleep again until he made sure.

Boot steps scraped at the dirt behind him, approaching with purpose but stopping at a respectful distance. Jed sussed who it was without looking. "He set a trap for us," he said to Cal.

Cal leaned against the wall and nodded. He fished a cigar stub from his pocket and struck a match. The man winced as he brought it up with his bad arm but managed the job.

"We were lucky it was just him," Cal said.

"Can't argue with you on that. I'll be ready for them next time, and with more men."

"You mean the reverend and the kid?"

"I mean getting a detachment sent from Fort Talbot."

"Past a blocked canyon and no railroad? That might take weeks, months even." Cal raised his brows and blew out a cloud of foul smoke. "We have to keep on the trail, Sheriff. Catch Pete and Braga before they make more of themselves and wipe out the entire valley."

"I'm with the sheriff," Hornsby called out as he sidled through the entryway. "We can't go after those monsters without overwhelming force."

Cal closed his eyes for a moment and took another drag. "Mayor, I won't call you yellow on account of you meeting the challenge when it came to it upstairs. But what you're saying right now comes awful close to the mark."

"We lost Porter," Hornsby said. "It took all of us to put down Bryan Carter, and we still lost Porter. What if Pete Carter had been with him? We need to wait for more men."

Cal waved the cigar at the shrouded bodies. "These homesteaders are dead because we didn't get here in time, Mayor," Cal said. "The whole valley could be wiped out in a week. "

Jed didn't know how it happened, but the surge bloomed in his chest, flowed through his arm, his fist, and then Cal was down, cigar skittering across the floor. Cal grunted as he landed on his bad shoulder, and he punched the floor as he swallowed a groan.

"My brother's dead because you cracked the seal on that devil's coffin," Jed said. "The only reason you're not laid out by the ashes of your friend is because I need every gun to see us through." Cal looked back with murder in his eye. Jed put a hand on his Peacemaker. "You're not as fast as you think, Trigger."

Cal's nostrils flared and for a moment, Jed thought he'd have to put the man down after all. But Cal let out his breath slow, and held up his hands, palms out. "We're on the same side, Sheriff, so I'm not going to hold a grudge, but that's the only free shot you get, because I know your head ain't in the right place just now."

"My head's just fine. We were lucky to kill that thing and only lose one man. Going up against two with the night coming ain't even worth considering."

"You've got the right of it, Sheriff," Hornsby said. Cal continued glaring, but he kept his mouth shut as he pushed to his feet.

"We're going back to town to warn the others and put my niece with family," Jed said.

"And what about the other families in the valley tonight?" Cal asked.

"They'll have to take their chances, just like they always have."

Cal turned on his heel and left the house, muttering.

"You made the right call, Sheriff. Some men have the luxury of not having to think about others." Hornsby said.

Jed flipped the blanket back over John's face. "We'll see, Mayor." He crossed to the corner and ground out the smoldering cigar. It wouldn't do to burn down John's house on account of an outlaw's vice.

They rode back to town in silence, more or less. What words were spoken were for the horses and the little girl in Jed's saddle that seemed to have drawn into herself, staring ahead. The mountain's shadows turned a deep purple above them as the sunlight disappeared, the cooling air around them tempered by heat radiating from the sand and rock at their feet.

Jed put them at a quick pace, driving the horses more than he'd have liked, but his mind turned every odd shape into twisted creatures lurking behind each darkened bush and boulder, or crouching in the trees overhead, calling to each other in coyote barks and crow's caws. The sooner he got the posse home, the better.

Molly shivered as full darkness fell. He had to tell Hornsby to keep his damn hands off his gun before he did something stupid. The man was jumping at shadows and spooking Sam as well. Cal just rode ahead, ready, senses alert, but even the hardened criminal glanced back along their trail when he thought Jed wasn't watching.

They approached Sunset's city limits. A howl pierced the night. Wood snapped, and horses whinnied. Cal and Jed shared a look, then a familiar woman's voice screamed. Jed shifted Molly to Reverend Graham and spurred Cactus to a sprint, wondering if he was already too late. Again.

Chapter Seventeen

Sarah was no expert on horses, but the whinnies and stamping from the livery gave her pause. Then the town's dogs started baying and she put back the bottle of a German digestive liquor she'd ordered long ago but no one had ever asked after. She poked her head outside the saloon's doors into the night's gloom, noting others doing the same down the street, all the way to the church at the far end. The last time the animals had been this riled up was that spring the bear came through town, skinny from winter and hungry as a boxcar of teenage boys. She went back to the bar and retrieved the double-barrel from under it. The shotgun wouldn't be any more use than her derringer against a bear, but the noise might well scare it off.

A howl broke through the night, and a shadow flickered in the corner of her eye above the telegraph office. She readied the shotgun. The shadow passed across the shingles, flowing along the roof like a wave. A wolf, she decided, until the bare-chested man stepped into the moonlight and howled again.

Sarah lowered the shotgun's barrel. "Peyote," she muttered. Or dope. Whiskey, perhaps but the man wasn't stumbling. Or just plain crazy from weeks of heat. She was feeling the urge to take a shot at him anyway just on general principles, but she resisted. It wouldn't help Jed's prospects with the governor if word got around she was some kind of wild woman.

Boards creaked, then snapped. The man dropped through the telegraph office roof and went on a tear inside. Papers swirled like a snowstorm around him, and metal screeched and clanked within its center. He was in trouble now, she thought. The railroad took their telegraph operations seriously.

She was about to call Deputy Otto when a discordant note twanged, and sparks flew from a swaying telegraph pole. Sarah's heart clenched.

"That idiot."

Well, it would hardly matter if she took a shot at him now. Word wouldn't get out until the wires were fixed, which wouldn't happen until the railroad bridge at the gorge opened or the rockslide blocking the pass was cleared. This might be her only chance to shoot a man and get away with it.

The telegraph office's door flew off its hinges and the man cackled as he strode from the ruined office and onto the street. His eyes found Sarah's and he grinned, white teeth gleaming. Sarah was stunned to recognize the man as the pushy cowboy from earlier, but something about him was different. He was still scrawny, still dirty, but his teeth certainly hadn't been that white, and he had an uncanny, dangerous vitality about him.

"How about that drink?" he said.

She brought the shotgun to her shoulder. "I hardly think so. Whatever you're on, I think you've had enough."

"Darlin', you don't know the half of it."

Deputy Otto finally got his fat ass unhitched from the jailhouse and shouted as he jogged down the boardwalk. The cowboy didn't pay him any mind, even when Otto pulled his revolver. He strutted, arrogant as a prize rooster, before leaping in a high arc from the middle of the street, straight at Sarah, arms wide, a maniacal grin on his face.

Sarah fired and ducked as the man sailed overhead, crashing into a table and sending beer bottles smashing to the floor. Sarah cocked the second barrel and advanced, but she was sure the man was down for good, having caught the first barrel's buckshot dead center. Gunpowder burned her nose, but the stench of him still cut through.

He lay on the slanting table, legs partially broken and pointing at odd angles. His chest was a mess, and Sarah swallowed back the remnants of dinner that wanted out. He wasn't dead yet, his chest still rose and fell, and her vision swam as the cowboy's tissues *moved* at the wound's edges.

He coughed. "That hurt."

"Well, it won't for much longer," she said.

He laughed, a hissing bubble that got stronger as she watched flesh pucker and seal the hole in his chest. He flipped to his feet and knocked the shotgun from her hands as she fired. Plaster rained down from the ceiling as he knocked her back into the wall, driving the wind from her lungs.

The cowboy let out another wolf howl, holding the shotgun by the barrel end and shaking it in the air. He turned his gaze back on her and held the gun before him. Muscle rippled and the barrel bent like taffy until the stock splintered and the cowboy tossed it aside. His eyes had a red tinge to them, not bloodshot, more like two fresh-lit cigars. Terror seized her chest and squeezed, leaving her lightheaded as blood thundered in her ears.

"Now, about that drink," he said, eyes shifting away from hers, down, fixing at her collarbone. Her vision wavered, the edges going gray as she tried and failed to remember how to breathe.

He took a step, panic turning her limbs to stone as a tongue lashed against monstrous canines. Her stomach twitched and fresh air rushed in.

The derringer came to hand.

The cowboy sneered.

She fired, shifted, fired again between heartbeats.

The cowboy screamed louder than a train whistle and his hands went to his face, watery blood streaming from ruined eyes. He lunged for her, long sharpened nails tearing at her hair and dress as she rolled aside. Her hand closed on a broken table leg, and she set herself as the claws scythed right and left.

Sarah stepped in and swung the club with all her might. The shock traveled down her arms and the wood fell from numbed fingers. The cowboy's head snapped sideways, then he stumbled over the table's remains onto the floor.

Sarah turned and ran for the exit, right into her husband. Jed looked like Jonah spit from the whale, but the world stopped spinning for a moment as their arms wrapped around each other. Otto pushed past them and Jed started barking orders.

"Flip him over and sit on him, Otto. Cal, you help. Sam, go to the smithy and get the heaviest chain you can find."

"You sumbitches are gonna be real sorry when I come free," the cowboy was saying.

"He's still alive?" Sarah said. "I hit him with a chest full of buckshot, and a .22 to each eye."

"Yeah, I've got something special planned for you, bitch," the cowboy said. His head turned and one eye, blood-filled but regrown, bored through her. The tall lanky stranger with Otto grabbed the cowboy by his greasy hair and thumped his skull into the floor three times. The man thrashed like a spooked bronco, but he couldn't throw off Otto and the stranger.

"Why is that man not dead?" she asked.

"Now's not the time," Jed said. His jaw had a clench that meant he was about to go all cold on her, stop being her husband and become Sheriff Scott once again. As if he couldn't do both things at once.

"He liked to have killed me, Jedidiah," she said.

"I'm relieved he didn't. His friends killed John and Caroline."

Sarah put her arms around him. "I'm sorry, Jed. Molly, too?"

He shook his head. "No, thank God. I brought her back with me."

Sarah looked at the struggling man on her bar room floor. "Then why is he still alive?"

"I don't know. It takes more than a few bullets to kill them."

She pushed away. "I mean, why haven't you killed him already? If you're not going to finish the job, then I am." She went to the bar, looking for another weapon.

"Not just yet, Sarah."

"What, you're going to wait for a judge or something? We're cut off, Jed. We need to see after our own."

"No, I don't believe he's what God would call one of his creations anymore. He's something else, and we need to learn more about his kind."

"What is he, Jed?"

He shook his head. "It's too bizarre."

"I think I deserve to know what you're not telling me, Jedidiah Scott. You're talking like there are more like him around, so if another one shows up, springs him loose? Then what?"

Jed winced. "It won't come to that. I've got a handle on this guy."

Sarah gestured to the wreckage, then pointed to the telegraph office. "How can you hold a man that can do all this?" She stopped to look at the cowboy pinned and struggling on the floor. "My God, you don't know how to kill him, do you?"

"We killed the one that got John, but there are others."

Sarah met Jed's grim look. "How many more, Jed? Two? A dozen? A hundred?" Her thoughts flew to Atticus and Melody asleep in their room with only a storekeeper's daughter keeping watch until the saloon closed for the night.

"At least two. But don't worry, I plan to get after them and hunt them down. I'll deputize more men and leave them with Otto to keep you safe."

She poked him in the chest. "You're going back out? I need you here. The town needs you here. Not Otto, not Sam. You."

"Don't tell me how to be a lawman, Sarah. I don't tell you how to run the saloon."

Sam came in, staggering under the weight of two heavy chain loops. The cowboy struggled until the stranger put a gun to his head and threatened to empty all six chambers. Sarah reckoned he had the right idea.

Sarah said, "They've got all the valley to hide in and circle around behind your back. We don't have enough eyes or guns to watch everything, and now we can't even call for help. All we have is us, Jed."

"The best way to deal with these things is to take the fight to them. Smoke 'em out and keep them on the move," Jed said.

"And what if they come here while you're out looking? What about Atticus and Melody? You want to orphan them just like Molly?"

Jed's eyes went distant, and Sarah knew she'd gotten him to see sense. Right up until that twitch in his jaw came back. That damnable twitch she'd found so thrilling when they were courting, but in the years since she'd come to resent. He'd made up his mind against her.

"I know what I'm doing."

The cowboy was hogtied with chains and was being dragged out by Otto and the stranger. It snapped at her with its jaws, looking less and less like a man and more like a beast. It stared at her over its shoulder as the men hauled it away, and Sarah found her hand at her throat.

"You'd better find them all and put them down, Jed. I don't know what you'll come home to if you're wrong."

Jed held his breath for a long moment before letting it out and clasping a rough hand over hers. "I know you're scared, Sarah."

"Terrified, more like, and not just for me. I used to think being a sheriff's wife was quite the feather in my hat. Now I'm not so sure."

He brought both hands to her shoulders and gave them a squeeze. "I'll see this through. And when it's done, we'll get the telegraph repaired, and the first message out will be to the governor's office, see if he still wants a marshal."

It was as much as he was going to budge for now, but she'd take it. Mountains could be moved, if only a little at a time. "I'll hold you to that, Jed."

He tipped his cap. "I wouldn't have it any other way."

Chapter Eighteen

JED CONTEMPLATED THE VAMPIRE LOCKED UP IN THE CELL. Or rather, the hogtied vampire wrapped in chains within the locked cell. Otto's never-ending pot of coffee had burnt Jed's tongue, and the muck left swirling in his tin mug now tasted like ashes. He drank it anyway. It was more important to stay alert and push through his fatigue while Cal, Sam, and Otto went about town gathering supplies for the morning's expedition. The vampire had stopped ranting about getting fed an hour back after he'd retched up a plate of beans put before him. Blood, he wanted, but Jed wasn't moved. The man — vampire, he corrected himself — had tried for his wife, which left Jed less than obligating. The vampire refused to answer questions, not even his name, Charlie Potter, which he'd learned from Cal. A Dust Crow, or former one, depending on how one looked at it. Ranting like a lunatic long into the night, but now had settled into some kind of half-sleep or palsy as dawn approached.

He should just kill the thing and put its soul out of

misery, assuming it had one anymore, but he needed to know where Braga, Pete, and the rest of the Dust Crows had run to. His wife would have him hunker down and let the vampires come to him, but she didn't know war like he did. The best way to keep the slow and inexperienced alive was to not have them face the danger at all. He was a cavalryman and learned early on that speed and maneuver were his greatest friends, especially against the untrained like all those blues back in the day, fleeing through the hills as he ran them down on horseback.

Out in the open, he could deal with these creatures. He'd just need to draw them out to a killing ground of his choosing.

Cal and Reverend Graham entered in with a wrapped bundle of sharpened wooden tent pegs. "The closest thing we have to what was sticking through Braga when we found him," Cal said. He looked to Charlie Potter in the cell. "We could test them out on that one."

Graham pursed his lips as he studied the vampire. "We should relieve Charlie's soul of its suffering."

"It's got information I need. Won't do to kill it," Jed said.

Cal shrugged. "If he won't talk, what use is he? Besides," he hefted his bundle, "sticking him with one of these might just be temporary. Kill him, pull it out, let him reform, and stake him if he won't answer. After a few goes, I bet he gets tired of it and 'fesses."

Jed took a slug of coffee and came up from the desk, brushing his hands. "Well, no sense in dawdling."

Cal unbundled the tent stakes, which were wrapped in canvas aprons. He handed an apron to Jed. "In case there's a mess."

"Thoughtful of you, Cal."

Graham blanched. "Gentlemen! Let us be clear. We are men of God, not barbarous Khans, taking sport in death."

"Does that mean you don't want an apron, Preacher?" Cal asked. "You ain't squeamish, are you?"

Graham shouldered past Cal. "Antietam, Chancellorsville, Manassas. I held the hands of countless boys and men as they breathed their last, bodies mangled by musket ball, cannon shot, saber slash, and the other ways man has turned his ingenuity to butchering his brother. I've held down men while the surgeon worked the bone saws and washed the foul ichor of wounds gone septic." He paused, then added, "You will note I wasn't the one vomiting at day's end." Cal's eyes narrowed, but Graham was unmoved.

"That's enough, Ellis," Jed said.

Graham inclined his head. To Cal, he said, "Squeamish? No sir. Merely experienced in the soul's coarsening that results from committing such acts."

Cal laughed. "Foul ichor? You must really pack in them pews, Preacher. Assuming they're not puking in the aisles."

They opened the cell door, but Potter didn't respond, apart from red-tinged eyes flicking to the movement, then slowly returning to stare straight ahead. The chains binding him jingled.

Before Jed could speak, Graham went to his knees before the vampire. "There's still time to repent, Brother Charles. Pray with me." He withdrew a tiny Bible from his pocket and closed his eyes to speak.

The vampire's face twisted, and it lunged at Graham, chains thrumming as they brought him up short of sinking jaws into the Reverend's neck. It screamed as Graham prayed, skin blistering and pustules exploding as if standing before a blast furnace. Graham screwed his eyes tighter and raised his voice over the din, invoking the familiar names and figures from Scripture, plus a few Jed didn't recall.

The vampire's pocked flesh turned black, a miasma of decay rose within the cell. The monster thrashed in its chains and looked to Cal, who held a stake in a white-knuckled grip.

"Wilson!" the vampire screeched. "They're at the Wilson house!"

Jed put a hand on Graham's shoulder. "Reckon that's enough saving for one day, Ellis."

Graham opened his eyes and took in the state of the vampire. He turned a calm gaze on Cal until the other man looked away, then rose to his feet and left the cell. The vampire slumped in its chains, twitching. Jed expected its skin to start regrowing, but it showed no sign.

They locked the cell door and retreated to the office. Cal found Otto's stashed whiskey bottle and took a long pull. Jed didn't begrudge the outlaw, though he'd made sure he didn't finish it off entire.

"The old Wilson place isn't far," Jed said.

Cal wiped the back of a hand across his mouth. "It's like to be falling apart."

"Then there won't be much cover for them. Punch a few holes and let the sunlight take care of the rest."

Jed nodded. "Assuming it's not another trap."

Cal jabbed a thumb to the cells. "I don't see how. This one wasn't going to talk until the Reverend tried saving its soul." He smiled at Graham, who shrugged as he helped himself to a coffee.

Cal swirled his mug as the thought. "Maybe it wasn't supposed to let the cat out of the bag until later."

"Then we'll catch them off guard, won't we?"

"That we might."

"All right," Cal said, and picked up a stake. "You going to just leave him here until the sun comes through the window, or should I stick him now?"

"I believe I can still save his soul," Graham said. "The light of the Lord will burn the corruption from him."

Cal sniffed. "And what if it's corruption all the way down?"

Graham leaned in. "He would never let such an abomination to exist, or else what hope have men like you?"

"You're asking for a fight, Reverend?"

"Striking me would only prove my point."

Cal shrugged and gave the stake a flip. "It might also make you shut up about things you don't know a thing about, Preacher."

Jed put a hand on Graham's shoulder and gently pulled him back from Cal. "We'll put it in a coffin and keep it locked up here."

THE SUN ROSE, and Jed deputized a few men before putting them under Otto to sharpen more tent stakes and make lances while Mayor Hornsby oversaw setting up barricades around town. When the people asked why, Jed and the Mayor were at a loss on how to explain something he almost didn't believe himself until Cal stepped in to tell the others the Dust Crows had stolen a cache of pistols and were coming to raid the town. The stakes would be placed in pits to take out their horses, something the Crusaders did against the Huns, or so he claimed, but the people nodded along and got to working, so Jed reckoned it didn't hurt them any even if it wasn't true.

When he was nearly saddled up, Sarah was there in the shadow of the saloon's awning, arms folded, and head cocked in that way Jed had come to associate with some unfathomable infraction on his part.

"I'll be back directly," he said to Sam and followed Sarah, who'd already disappeared into the saloon.

Chapter Nineteen

JED PUSHED THROUGH THE SALOON'S BATWING DOORS AND strode past the bar, maneuvering around a gathered pile of broken furniture and plaster chunks. The day man, Holder, looked up from his sweeping and jerked his head towards the back office. Jed nodded and made his way there, boots clomping against the floorboards. He pushed the door open and found his wife studying a woodcut of a London promenade, shoulders tight, arms wrapped around her stomach.

"Your boots make enough noise to wake the dead," she said.

Jed smiled. "No one ever accused me of sneaking around on my wife," he said.

She sniffed. "No, never that. Though I expected you to be out of town by now."

"I brought you this." Jed held out his Sharps rifle.

Sarah glanced at the gun, then back at the woodcut. "A buffalo gun? I would think you'd be wanting that out on your hunt."

"A derringer and double-barrel are fine for handling

drunks and such, but that thing you faced last night? I'll feel better if I knew you had this."

"Will it truly make a difference?"

"It's been blessed by the reverend. Holy words seem to impart a mighty effect."

"Perhaps I should arm myself with a Bible, then."

"Maybe. There's a lot we don't know."

Sarah turned. "All the more reason for you to stay, Jed."

Jed ran a hand down the Sharp's solid stock. "If the blessing don't take one of them things down, this thing has enough kick to knock them off their feet. Long enough for you to get a wooden stake in 'em or run away." When she didn't reach for it, he took a step closer and pressed it into her arms. "Please. Take it and get back to the house. The saloon's got too many ways in. Lock the doors, shutter the windows, and keep Atticus, Melody, and Molly safe until I get back. And I will come back, I promise."

She sighed and took the rifle. "You can't promise that."

"A vow, then. I have to go, Sarah. These creatures need to be put down. Their souls are stained. It'll fester all the worse if I don't."

"You took a vow to me, Jedidiah Scott, remember?"

"I do."

She sniffed and shook her head. She set the rifle aside and grabbed his face with both hands, pulling it down to hers and planting a soft kiss on his lips. He reached for her, but she pushed him away.

"No. If you want more, it will have to wait until you come back."

Jed straightened and fought the urge to pick her up and steal another kiss while she was distracted, but Sarah seemed to know what he was thinking and raised an eyebrow. Jed knew he was beaten, so he touched his hat's brim and took his leave.

~

Outside town, Jed scanned the hills for movement, trying to recall what he knew about the Wilson house. Cal was telling some tall tale to Sam, making the younger man guffaw with each more unlikely detail. He even got old Quinn McCarthy, the town farrier and Porter's second cousin, to grin. Jed had given the outlaw his gun rig back, an odd threesome of matched Navy .36s and a baby Patterson, which he claimed was the best of all worlds. When pressed on what worlds, Cal just winked. For himself, Jed was glad to have his Starr on the other side of his Peacemaker. His loaning it to Cal had made him feel unbalanced.

Reverend Graham's mule trotted up alongside his own.

"Sheriff."

"Reverend."

Graham took a moment to doff his hat and wipe his brow. "Normally this is the time of day I would pray to the Lord for rain. However, I see now that in his wisdom, he has provided us with another clear day for our endeavor."

"I won't complain, Reverend, that's for sure."

They rode on for a spell, then a thought came to Jed.

"You reckon you made the right choice coming along? Don't get me wrong, I'm mighty grateful for your help, but shouldn't you be seeing to your flock?"

"I could ask the same of you."

Jed shook his head. "Whether it's the right or wrong decision, I've already made it and won't know of its wisdom until everything's over."

Graham shifted in his saddle and gave Jed an

appraising look. "The clergy are often cast as shepherds, which doesn't say much about the congregation, does it? And yet the shepherd is often beholden to the master of the farm, responsible and having to answer for the fate that befalls the sheep, because the shepherd is gifted with knowledge and tools that the sheep lack."

"I never was much for farming, Reverend. What's your point?" Jed asked.

"If the sheep could protect themselves, they would not need us, but they cannot, so we must. And sometimes when there are wolves in the hills, the shepherd cannot go back to the master and ask what should be done, for that would be leaving the flock undefended. Likewise, waiting for the wolves to attack before taking action would require sacrificing at least one of the flock. The best way to save them all is to kill the wolves before they attack, or hope to chase them away."

"So long as the wolves aren't circling around when the shepherd is getting lost in the hills, but that's why we left the dogs behind."

"Otto might not take kindly to being called a dog," Graham said.

"I'm sure he's been called worse. How about you, Reverend? Are you a shepherd or sheep dog?"

Graham's chortle rumbled. "Oh, I'm very much the dog. If you'll recall the Psalms, 'The Lord is my shepherd,' there's no mention about Ellis Graham that I've ever discovered."

THEY STOPPED MIDWAY to the ranch for a brief rest when the horses startled and pulled at their leads. Cal shouted and slung a rock into the bushes. A streak of black fur emerged and dashed off.

"Coyote?" Jed called out.

"Damned big one if it were. Wolf, maybe?" Cal said.

McCarthy shook his head. "Had to be a wild dog. Wolves are too smart to bother men."

Cal shrugged. "Big son of a bitch either way." He walked to Rocky and started talking softly to him, steadying his head as he tugged at his bridle.

Jed found the best way to settle horses was to get them moving. Men, too, for that matter. "Mount up," he said. He had the feeling of eyes on his back, an itch at the back of his neck, and turned, but couldn't find the source.

"Something?" Cal asked.

"Can't say," Jed replied and looked for the hills for a man's outline or a flash of glass.

Cal twisted to look around and winced, pressing a hand to his shoulder. "I'll hurry them up," he said.

The posse headed out, riding closer than usual. The itch at the back of his neck remained, and it didn't take long before he spotted the spooked wolf. Black furred, skinny, but still half again larger than any dog Jed had ever seen. It shadowed them a few hundred yards out on his left, glancing at them every so often and giving Jed the unnatural feeling of being something's meal.

"Sheriff," Sam said.

"I see it."

"Want, I could ride it down. Scare it off." He said it offhand, trying to be casual. Trying to sound like Cal, Jed realized. He didn't need that attitude from his deputies.

"Hold for now, Deputy Perkins," Jed said, confident the young man would catch his drift.

"There's another one," Cal said, and nodded to the

right. Jed found another wolf, gray-faced, pacing their other flank. "They can't think they can take us."

"They're desperate, more like. Hoping for someone dropping out sickly or lame." Jed felt the shift in Cactus's gait, a nervous flutter that told him the horse knew the wolves were about. Thankfully Cactus couldn't smell them.

"We can outrun 'em," Sam said.

"Horses can. Don't know about Graham's mule."

Graham patted his mount's neck. "Don't worry about Sacks, she's got it in her," he said.

Jed squinted and turned back to the trail. "They're still keeping their distance for now. We keep moving."

As the afternoon wore on, more wolves joined in singles and pairs, until a good dozen were spread out to their flanks and behind. Jed had the group take up the pace, but the pack kept up, and now Cactus had a tremor fluttering and was tiring himself out. Graham's mule kept up, Jed had to admit, but it grew increasingly squirrelly under the reverend. The men were scarcely better, variously trying to keep the predators at bay with shouting, suddenly veering towards the closest animal and firing warning shots. Individual wolves would scurry or shy away for a spell, but inevitably rejoined the pack within minutes.

Then Jed spotted the biggest pair emerging from the bushes dead ahead. Yellow eyes over white and gray muzzles met his. They ran straight at him, low to the ground with fangs bared. The horses panicked, scattering the posse. Cactus reared and Jed fell forward, clinging to the saddle.

Graham's mule cried out and bolted, taking the reverend with him.

Jed got Cactus under control and turned after the retreating Graham. The pack flowed after the mule, more than Jed had realized had been following.

"After him!" he shouted.

He put the spurs to Cactus with a light touch, just to give the animal some focus. The pack nipped at the mule's rear flanks, barking and snarling. Sacks bayed and lashed out with a hoof, catching one of its attackers in the ribs and drawing a pained yip. Jed drew his Starr and took aim at a brindle-coated wolf gathering itself. Cactus stayed steady as the gun went off and the bullet caught the wolf in mid-leap. It twisted and its jaws fell short of the mule's hindquarters, but claws raked bloody furrows.

Graham bounced and tried grabbing at loose reins, jerking fingers back from snapping jaws as the pack came at him from the front.

Cal fired again, taking out a black-coated wolf streaking in from the left. More gunfire behind him. Jed tried keeping Cactus on a straight line and prayed the guns behind him aimed true and he wouldn't catch a stray in the spine.

The pack scattered and Jed caught up to Graham. The preacher's fingers finally wrapped around the reins, and Jed put Cactus close to Sacks in hopes the horse's presence would calm the mule down some. Graham pulled on the reins and shouted "woah" at the mule. Between the presence of Cactus and Graham's oratory, Sacks slowed, then came to a stop.

Jed grinned down at Graham. "What was that about wolves, shepherds, and sheepdogs, Reverend?"

Graham shook his head vehemently. "Blast my tongue for its pride!"

The wolves gathered behind them, the two largest at the vanguard. Jed pulled his Winchester from Cactus's saddle scabbard and took aim at the largest white one. It lowered its head as he lined up the sights and seemed to dare Jed. He squeezed the trigger, and the ground before the animal puffed up. Missed. He forgot the Winchester had a touch of left drift. He had gotten too used to the Sharps, else it would have been a different story. The wolf turned tail and ran, taking the rest of the pack with him.

The rest of the posse pulled up.

"You all right?" Cal asked Graham.

"Sacks here has some scrapes and gouges, but fortunately escaped getting hamstringed. I'm afraid she's blown."

Jed ran a gloved hand through the lather on his horse's skin and frowned. Cactus's flanks were working like a bellows as well. "We'll have to take another rest, or they'll be no good once we get to the Wilson place."

"Those gunshots will carry on the wind. Chances are anyone there will have heard all this commotion, too," Cal said.

Jed took off his hat and bashed it against his thigh twice before resetting it on his head. "Can't be helped. Damn it to hell, but it can't be helped."

Chapter Twenty

CAL HAD VISITED THE ABANDONED WILSON PLACE ONCE before when the Six had been looking for a hideout. The ranch had been built before the railroad had come through, back when the wagon trails were king, and had much to offer with a big house and barns along with good sight lines to the approaches. It would have been a damn sight more hospitable than where they'd ended up, but they had rejected it for the same reason its owners had left — no water. The once majestic trees along the old stream bed were twisted leafless things, too rooted in the hard ground to fall and too dry to rot away. The cattle pastures were as blasted and rocky as the trail had been, with only the occasional juniper or creosote bushes still making a go of it among the yellow and brown scrub of dead spring growth.

The house itself was still intact, and in better shape than Cal's hideout even though it'd been built a good ten years later. The graying wood still had traces of lemony yellow paint, and the shingled roof hadn't a single hole in it. Stone chimneys, wide as two men, bookended the home like castle turrets and gave it a solid presence that must have made old man Wilson believe it would stand for generations.

The sheriff's repeater sat across his saddle as he surveyed the place with a frown. Cal wondered if Jed saw his dead brother's home. Unlike the farmstead, the place hadn't any livestock in the barns, no dead bodies in the yard, or curtains in the windows. The afternoon's heat soaked through him as the air stilled, and Cal gave his nearly empty canteen a shake before deciding he may as well finish it off.

"What do you reckon, Cal?" Jed said. "They got something waiting for us?"

"If they're even there. Lots of places to hide and ambush, but also not a lot of cover for them if they get flushed out. It's gonna be a shame."

Jed blinked. "A shame?"

"You recall what Sherman did to Atlanta?"

Jed shook his head. "We need to know if they're inside first. Fan out, but keep in sight of each other, and in the sun. Holler if you see anything."

Cal shrugged and took the left flank. He guided Rocky at a trot and pictured the ranch's layout in his head. If Pete were in charge, what traps would he set? Would he have dynamite charges planted in the barns? A sharpshooter in a darkened window? How much sun could Pete tolerate as one of those vampire things?

He didn't believe Pete could be anything other than that now, given what happened with Bryan. If nothing else, each brother couldn't stand not having something the other had.

The barn doors were wide open, showing nothing but dirt floor and empty stalls. Likewise with the smoke house and corral. The more he thought of it, the more he believed Pete was in the house. He could almost see himself atop Rocky as Pete would. He could imagine Pete's resentment and simmering frustration coming to boiling under a tight lid of patience with a dash of cowardice, waiting for Cal to step foot in his trap. He imagined Pete wanted Cal to just die already so he could step out of Cal's shadow, so to speak.

Cal laughed to himself at that. Pete wouldn't be stepping out into the light anytime soon.

THEIR SWEEP TURNED up empty buildings. They weren't willing to enter the house, but looking through the open windows showed them nothing but an empty house so far.

"That Potter fella sold us a pig in a poke," Sam said.

"Might be, but it's a funny thing to make up when your skin's melting off," Cal said.

"I would imagine a man will say anything he thinks will make the agony stop," Graham said.

"If Potter is even a man anymore, Reverend. Who's to say?"

Jed chopped the air with a hand. "We still need to search the house and be sure," he said.

"Then what are we waiting for?" McCarthy asked.

Cal took a glance at the front door and felt a chill run him through. "I don't fancy going in there. I still say setting fire to it is the way to go."

McCarthy laughed. "The mighty Trigger Jones. You'd rather shoot someone in the back to a straight-up fight?"

Cal tightened his grip on the saddle horn. "You want, we can try it, you and me. I'll even let you draw first."

Jed's horse pushed between them, but the sheriff's eyes never left the house. "Knock it off, McCarthy. You don't know what you're talking about."

"But Sheriff—"

"But nothing, McCarthy." Jed nodded and then eyed the sun. "I wonder if they heard us coming and ran."

"They can't just run during the day though, right? Maybe they're holed up, playing possum in some closet or pantry."

"Be best if we just burned the whole thing down," Cal said.

"Won't Wilson's kin mind?"

Cal shrugged. "They had all this time to come out and claim it. We'll just tell 'em it was lightning or brushfire that did it."

"Only one problem," Jed said. "There's a root cellar. Opens to the yard and the house."

"How you know?" McCarthy asked.

Jed spared a glance at Cal. "Place like this would make a fine hideout. I could see a famous band of outlaws setting up digs here, apart from the lack of water, that is."

"That so, Sheriff?" Cal said, silently thanking the luck of idiots the Six hadn't settled here after all.

Jed shrugged. "A man'd have to scout it out to be sure, so I took a look around once upon a time."

McCarthy grinned from ear to ear as Cal shifted in the saddle. "And what'd you find?"

Jed shrugged. "That even if the house collapses in, it might not bury the cellar. And if I was looking for the darkest place in the house, that's where I'd be."

Jed's mouth twisted. Sam looked like he'd just swallowed a toad.

Jed nodded along. "Yeah, I feel like going down there even less than the front door."

"We'll start the fire down there," Cal said. "Stuff it full of kindling and let the flames rise."

"Might not need all that much," Jed said. "Wilson had

a stockpile of kerosene in the basement. Some of it still might be there if the cans haven't rusted away.

Sam swallowed. "And if Braga and Pete Carter are down there with a few Crows?"

"Then we'll stay outside in the light."

THEY CHOPPED branches loose from the dead trees in short order, stacking them outside the root cellar's outer door, dug below ground level near one of the chimney's foundations. Graham went from man to man, saying a prayer over their weapons and spare bullets. Cal sharpened a few of the cut ends on the branches into crude points and made sure each man had one.

"Braga had one of these pinning him down in that coffin. We see him and his down there, we might need to do the same if the bullets run out."

Jed lined them up. "Cal, you're in the lead. Sam, you back him up, Then me and the reverend will follow. McCarthy, you hang back and make sure the door stays open behind us. We see Braga, Pete Williams, or any of them Crows, retreat. Got it?"

Everyone nodded, and Jed grasped Cal by his good shoulder. "Ready, Cal?"

Cal smirked. "Probably nothing down there but an old pickle jar," he said, but when he set his boot on the first step, he felt time stretch and a lump of ice settle in his stomach. The gray door looked solid enough, though its crude wooden handle held on by rusted nails didn't fill him with confidence. Like as not, it'd come off in his hand.

No, that was just fear fucking with him. The longer he waited, the more the others would wonder if Trigger Jones had finally lost his nerve. He took in a slow breath, then spared a glance over his shoulder at Sam. Lord, the kid looked scared.

Cal let the breath out as he yanked on the handle. The wood resisted for only a moment, then came free with a screech. Cal pushed his gun forward, looking for targets. The cellar was pleasantly cool, but smelled of earth, kerosene, and rust. He ducked under the low ceiling, swinging a gun left and right. Sam shoved him from behind, then surprised him by uttering a halfway decent rebel yell. They pushed into the gloom and Cal sensed Braga nearby, just like the nightmare, with a dread that pushed the air from his lungs and set his legs numb.

More footsteps behind him.

Jed and Graham's shadows fell across the doorway, the Reverend reciting Scripture as he descended, full of "thees" and "thous" for good measure.

A rustle from the right.

A gleam of red within a shadow moved, and Cal fired.

The flash revealed three fanged Crows rushing in. The bullet took the nearest and sent him to his knees. More gunfire from his left as the kid opened up. Powder flashes lit the back of the cellar, picking out a tall, lean figure near the stairway wearing a heavy moldering carpet like a cloak.

Cal fired twice. The Crow he had hit before was still down on a knee with fingers digging the sizzling bullet from its chest. Maybe the reverend's blessed bullets were worth a pinch after all. But it wouldn't be enough. They were outnumbered at least five to four.

He tapped Sam on the shoulder twice. "Back out!" he shouted.

They retreated to the edge of the sunlight on the dirt floor. A taloned hand reached for him and Jed's shot came over his shoulder, dropping a Crow hiding behind a timber footing.

Where's Pete? Cal wondered.

Another vampire lunged from the gloom, jerking short as Graham brandished his Bible at it. It lunged again, skin blistering, talons reaching to knock the Bible from the reverend's hand. Graham turned aside and his litany faltered as the talons dug into his forearm. Jed fired, and the vampire's head snapped back. Jed put himself in front of Graham, pistol in each hand.

"Outside! Outside!" McCarthy yelled.

A lariat flew in just as Sam took another step back. Sam yelped as he tripped, then shrieked as the loop cinched and jerked him into the shadows.

Cal was already grasping Sam's hand, pulling him back into the light. Jed hooked an arm under Cal's shoulder and pulled with him, though even with his help it felt like pulling against a draft horse. Sam's screams pitched higher, and his head started thrashing from side to side. Fresh blood sprayed into the light, and then a wet snap. The three men fell backwards. The kid's eyes bulged at the bloody remains of his leg, raggedy pant leg slack below the knee. Then his eyes rolled up into his head and he passed out.

Cal put a shoulder under Sam and heaved while Jed filled the air with lead. McCarthy was there in the doorway, waving them along and firing his pistol over their heads. Sam's dead weight eased as Graham took the deputy's other shoulder and they made for the exit with Jed right behind them.

The house groaned, and the dirt below Cal's boots trembled. Fine dust rained down on McCarthy, who looked up and froze a moment before a rock the size of a bull's head cut his cry short More rocks and mortar rained down as the chimney collapsed and cut off the sun.

When the rumbling stopped, Cal, Jed, Graham, and

Sam were left in a spotty semicircle of sunlight poking through hand-sized gaps in the rubble. Red-eyed vampires pressed at the edges, snapping and reaching around the sunbeams, hissing and snatching their hands away as they tried and failed to reach them.

Boots descended the stairs and Pete's voice called out from the back of the cellar as the Crows retreated. "How you like that one, Cal?" he asked. "Didn't need dynamite, just a strong push."

Rocks spilled into the cellar along with McCarthy, buried to the hips under the rubble. Cal pushed back to the man while he reloaded his pistols by touch.

"Lacks some elegance, if I gotta be honest," Cal said. He peered into the darkness, seeing if he could pick Pete out. The shadows stirred, a few glimpses of red eyes, edging along the walls. "Can I ask you a question, Pete?"

"Sure, Cal. What's on your mind?" the voice moved around. Pete wasn't going to let Cal get a fix on him. He noted his left Navy needed reloading and holstered it.

"Why'd you and Bryan cut out?"

Pete had moved a little to the right. "Lord Braga gave us a better offer."

Jed tried shifting the rock to get McCarthy free, but the farrier grunted in pain. "They're both broke, Sheriff," he said through clenched teeth.

"Keep him talking," Jed whispered. He moved on to Sam, wrapping the kid's belt above the gory stump and cinching it tight.

Cal's left hand reached past the stake tucked in his belt and drew his baby Patterson. "Better offer? Didn't work out so well for your brother."

"Fuck you, Trigger."

"And why am I talking to you and not this Braga fella?

That is who I saw wearing the carpet, yeah? I thought you wanted to be the boss."

"Lord Braga doesn't speak to peasants," Pete sneered.

Cal spared a glance back, noting Jed was trying to wrap Sam's stump while the kid was still passed out, his skin going waxy. "That's gotta be a problem when you're surrounded by Crows and shit-for-brains Williams," he said.

The light grew brighter. At first Cal thought it was the sun, then he realized it was coming from his left. Graham was praying over McCarthy, the cross embossed on his Bible giving off a silvery light. Muttering came from the darkness, along with more scuffling and the scraping of bone on bone.

"You know what I think, Pete?"

"Don't care, Trigger."

"I think Braga can't speak English, at least not yet. It's gotta chafe your ass that you're taking orders from a musty German fella."

"Maybe if you're lucky he'll make you like he made me, Trigger. But if he does, you can be damn sure you'll be licking the grave dust off my boots every evening until the end of time."

A harsh bark silenced Pete, followed by a low murmuring that Cal couldn't follow.

Pete called out again, as the murmur continued. "Lord Braga is generous. If you lay down arms now, he will show you the mercy you sure as shit don't deserve."

"That what he just said?" Cal asked.

"More or less." Pete grunted in pain and apologized as the murmuring took on a more ominous tone. "You've got wounded men," Pete continued more carefully. "Accept Lord Braga's offer and all will survive, restored to full … vitality. Forever young and strong."

"You gotta give us a moment, here, Pete," Cal said.

"Lord Braga has all the time in the world, but not infinite patience. You're trapped with no way out. Join or die, Trigger, it's just that simple."

Jed crouched next to Cal, but kept his eyes fixed on the walls and the creeping vampires. "We can't move McCarthy, and Sam is gonna bleed out."

"Y'all are going to have to get on without me," McCarthy said.

"We'll figure something out," Jed said. "I won't leave you, Quinn."

"Even Pete's gonna get tired of hearing the sound of his own voice," Cal said.

"I mean it, Sheriff. Just leave me with a loaded gun, maybe a cigar," McCarthy said.

Jed set his jaw and nodded, handing over Sam's revolver.

"May the Lord accept you directly into his arms, Brother Quinn," Graham said.

Cal lit a cigar and placed it between McCarthy's teeth. "When you're finished with that, reckon you can follow up with one of these." He handed over a stick of dynamite and his matchbox.

McCarthy puffed and nodded. "I'll give you the time I can."

"Think you can clear a path to the stairs?" Jed said.

Cal gripped both his guns. "Wouldn't change my mind even if we couldn't."

Jed nodded. "Right. Graham, you keep up showin' them the Good Book. Cal and I will take Sam between us."

Graham emerged, chanting the fire and brimstone better than any revival preacher Cal had ever had the misfortune to pass by. The silver glow coming off the Bible brightened as they approached the vampires, shielding their eyes as they retreated. Cal spied Pete disappearing deeper into the cellar's shadows, and Braga not at all.

Sam felt dangerously light on his shoulder. They rushed for the stairs, and Cal fired at movement to his left. Something hissed and he pushed Graham faster. The vampires were backing away from the pastor, circling behind and trying to get at them from where the silver light couldn't reach.

Fangs sank into Cal's leg, and he fired twice, feeling the impacts shudder up his leg as the vampire held on like a pit bull. He holstered the gun and grasped the sharpened stake from his belt and stabbed down, piercing through the monster's back and scraping across a rib. The vampire gasped like an old man and let go of his leg, while its hands flailed trying to reach the stake and pull it free.

Jed was shouting his name with guns barking and the next thing Cal knew, he was limping up the stairs with Sam, while Jed guided Graham backwards one step at a time as the preacher held his Bible out with both hands.

Cal's leg throbbed and he lost his balance. He pitched forward and bumped into Jed's back. Sam tumbled past him, over the stair's open edge and into the darkness, where two vampires fell on him like starving rats. The preacher faltered, and Jed took a step forward, but Cal grabbed both men by their collars and pulled them up the stairs.

"He's gone, Jed!"

Cal thought the sheriff was going to fight him on it, but he retreated up the last step with Cal and covered Graham as he passed the doorway, shooting a vampire running up the stairs when the silver light faded.

The men slammed the door with Graham and Jed holding it shut, while Cal searched for a barricade to drag across it. Cal could imagine McCarthy in the darkness, eyeing the dynamite by his cigar's orange glow….

The house didn't have much, but he spied a carved stump in the next room and dragged the heavy thing back to help jam the door.

The door surged and banged from the other side, but with the help of the stump, it held. Time sped up. Cal's stomach churned.

He didn't see Jed's fist until it was too late. "You dropped him, you sonovabitch!"

"Gentlemen!" Graham said.

Cal rubbed his jaw and picked himself up. "It wasn't on purpose, Jed! We can have it out later, but we need to move!"

"He was just a kid," Jed said.

"He was already dead, or near enough anyway."

Jed put a hand on his gun, and Cal knew he was going to catch a bullet. Running footsteps saved him.

The cellar door opened enough for a taloned hand to reach through and grab Graham by the shoulder. The reverend shoved his Bible into the gap and started preaching when he tripped over the stump and fell, wedged half in, half out of the stairwell.

Cal grabbed the man's feet and hauled back while Jed brought his guns to bear. Gunfire erupted over Graham's screams, and the door slammed shut. Graham fell to the floor, his right arm a ragged bloody stump. Warm blood pulsed, splattering his face. Cal reached out and pinched the slippery wound shut as best he could. Jed somehow got them both onto their feet just as the floor lifted and the door exploded from its hinges. The floorboards buckled and holes gaped with views into a cellar turned into a hellscape.

Burning kerosene engulfed a screaming vampire and

was already licking several other canisters. The vampires briefly forgot about Cal and the others as they scrambled like drowning rats to climb out of the cellar without getting caught in the open, the stronger holding the weaker before them as shields to take the brunt of the sun's fading light.

Cal and the others stumbled from the house, ears ringing. Cal wrapped and stuffed Graham's arm as tight as he could, then set making a tourniquet around the shoulder with the reverend's belt and a stake.

"He ain't gonna make it to Sunset," Cal shouted. "We'll have to ride for Buzby's."

Graham roused and looked wide-eyed at his missing limb. "Where did it go? We have to go back for it."

"Like hell, preacher," Cal said.

"I don't know if I can ride," Graham said.

"We'll rope you into the saddle if we have to, but you're going to live, Reverend." Jed grasped a fistful of hair and pulled the man's head up to face him. "You hang on, Ellis, you hear?"

Jed got them on horseback, and they thundered off to the shrieks of the burning vampires that went silent as a pillar of flame erupted, spreading to the outer walls and turning the old Wilson place into a fiery carnation.

Chapter Twenty-One

Buzby's Outpost looked no better in the dark than it did in daylight. The tilting, jagged roofline was set to fall over any day now, a mess of boards scavenged over the years from failed ranches, trading posts, and broken wagons. Many of the latter were still scattered around the property like stripped carcasses, a warning for travelers both coming and going. The only reason it hadn't succumbed to Sunset Valley's harsh climate and economic maladies was its location along the southern wagon trail at the high desert's edge, its deep well out back, and the orneriness of Buzby himself.

Cal checked on Sacks and her rider, tied in the saddle. Reverend Graham was feverish, muttering and crying out in fear, twice shouting in anger at whatever visions tortured him behind closed eyes. The man's voice cut through the chill air as Cal and Jed pushed their animals through the night. The mumblings of Graham's visions sounded an awful lot like the ones Cal saw on the back of his own eyelids. He wondered if there was a poison in vampire claws that affected men's brains, like hydrophobia and such. Were he and the preacher dead men walking?

No. Hell if he was. He touched two fingers to Jenny's cross and shook the thoughts off. They were being followed; both he and Jed could feel it. Neither man wanted to be caught in the open when whatever pursued them caught up.

"We're here, preacher," he said to Graham. "Hold on."

Buzby's place, for all its seedy atmosphere and remote location, was never empty and tonight was no exception as Cal counted six heads on his right, all in various drunken states looking up as he entered with Graham over his shoulder. Four horses blinked back at him over the half wall to his left. He ducked the low beam tied with the sage bundles Buzby used on account of the horse shit in the air and followed Cal as he headed for the table farthest from the horses and laid the preacher across it.

Buzby, a fat and balding man, blew out a drooping mustache and hitched his stained canvass trousers up to his prodigious belly. Beady eyes squinted, appraised, and likely knew how much money Cal and Graham had between them down to the penny. Buzby wasn't a greedy man, but he wasn't given to sentiment, either, nor could he be cowed. Every service had a price commiserate with the risk to Buzby's tiny kingdom and its monarch.

"You friend can't sleep there," Buzby said. "Paying customers only."

He blanched as Jed stepped fully into the lantern's light, the man's badge doubtlessly flashing bright. "Sheriff Scott," he said. Cal was chagrined at the fear and awe in Buzby's voice, a tone he never used with Cal, even with a gun in his face.

"Buzby, I got a wounded man and a whole lotta disagreeables coming after him."

"I don't want no trouble," Buzby said and hid something under the bar.

"You've got some, wanting or not. Where's your stove?"

Buzby jerked his head towards the back. Jed nodded and looked around the place, jaw working. He turned and addressed the room as he walked. "Men, consider yourselves all deputized. Cal will fill you in on the rest."

Heads turned to Cal. Blinked. "Whazzy talking about?" someone slurred.

Cal took a look around and knew the truth just wouldn't do. "Well boys, it's like this. We got ourselves some trouble the sheriff needs extra hands for, starting with saving the Reverend Graham here."

"What kind of trouble?" someone asked.

"The kind you better sober up for," Cal snapped. "I ain't got time for oratory. Help me clear some space!"

The drunks weren't much use moving tables, but when they got a closer look at Graham and his wounds, the questions stopped. Cal came back with a bucket of hot water and a glowing iron pipe. Cal pushed the flutter in his guts aside and started wrapping a bit of leather around a wooden peg.

"You know what you're doing?" he asked Jed.

Jed lowered his voice. "Seen it done, more like. Rather have the doc here, but I don't see us having the luxury. You hold him down."

Cal set the leather-wrapped peg between Graham's teeth and pressed his forearms on Graham's shoulders.

Buzby trundled up, saw what was about the happen, and got over his fear of Sheriff Scott, spluttering, "You can't do that here!"

"Buzby, you hold his legs," Cal said.

"Like hell."

Cal held up the glowing brand. "You want a man of God to die under your roof? Bad for business. Real bad. All that attention might look into corners you'd rather they didn't."

Buzby glowered, but then reached out, leaning his considerable bulk across Graham's thighs.

Cal had seen his share of nasty wounds, and since he wasn't acting as the sawbones, figured it would be best if he focused on Graham's face.

"We're gonna fix you up, preacher, get you back to saving souls in two shakes."

Graham's mumbling trailed off into a whisper. Cal leaned closer.

"...coming. Scrabbling over the ground on all fours, scenting blood like wolves. Bits of my arm stuck between their teeth. Driven like feral apes because they fear the voice in the shadow behind them. Driven by a hunger that will not slake."

Cal felt the man's forehead. Clammy with sweat yet cold as winter. "It's okay, Graham. We're safe here, miles ahead of them." But he could feel that same echo in his own mind. It was like he and Graham were watching the same macabre play or dreaming the same dream. That dream bloomed, coloring vivid inside his skull. A man, hungry like he hadn't eaten in weeks, loping down the trail in the moonlight. It could smell the horses, the men, the blood. It remembered being a man. It had a name, once. Creeping Rory.

"What's his name, Reverend?" Cal asked.

"Creeping—"

The Reverend screamed as the brand hit flesh. Cal turned away from the man's contorted features and the stench of charred meat. The faces of Buzby's motley patrons also turned aside, one man puking a sour mess on the floor. Graham went limp. Cal thanked the Lord on the reverend's behalf. While he wasn't on the greatest terms with the man upstairs himself, he reckoned it would probably be all right.

"He going to pull through, Jed?" Cal asked.

Jed gave the brand a wiggle and grimaced. "Near as much as I can tell. Let's hope Ellis is on better terms with the Lord than I am being a doctor. Bleeding's stopped anyways. It's up to Him from here." He held out a hand and Buzby handed him a bottle. Jed took a swing, then poured it on the wound. Cal took a pull of it himself, sour, acrid, and burning a path down his throat, before handing the bottle back to Buzby.

"Smooth," he said.

Buzby just glowered at him. "Two bits."

"I'll pay you tomorrow." Then to Jed, "They're on the trail. Be here soon."

Jed took in the crowd. "You get them organized, I'll get Ellis cleaned up and situated."

Cal looked around and didn't like their chances, the room already skittish and rattled. What would convince these skinny cowards to stand and fight rather than turning tail? He racked his brains for a believable, compelling lie.

He pointed to Graham and called out so they could hear him in the corners. "Brother Graham just ran afoul a particularly ornery Apache war band while baptizing the chief's daughter in the light of the Lord. Took a hatchet to his arm, and well… Anyway, they're likely following the blood trail and will be here directly. The sheriff's asking you all to take up arms against the heathens, which I expect will turn back once we put the issue to 'em with a little help from Misters Winchester and Colt."

"The Army chased the last Apache out a decade

back," someone said. "Just before the railroad came through."

"I thought the same," Cal said. "But it's hard to argue with a missing arm."

"And they cut if off for baptizing the chief's daughter?" said someone else. A woman, he realized.

Cal looked to the unconscious preacher. What the man couldn't hear wouldn't hurt him. Cal shrugged and let his lips curl into a smirk. "Well, he said he was baptizing her. Didn't see the act itself."

Someone else snorted. "Wonder if he was using some other limb, but the Apaches found it too hard to reach from horseback."

"Too small a target," the woman said.

A few snickered, and Cal just smiled along now that he had them. He cast his eyes around. The trading post was sod construction, dried mud and grass layered and held together with rough-hewn wood posts and repurposed pallets. The roof was surprisingly solid, but maybe that was just his own being used to a rickety barn.

"Best shore up the weak spots, boys," he said. It wasn't a bad place to hold out from an attack, though he wished it were Apaches coming. He would have liked their chances better.

Chapter Twenty-Two

Jed wondered what life would have been like if he had taken to the cloth, wondered if it would have been him lying all pale, sweaty, and missing an arm but blissfully unaware of death circling outside. He wondered if he would have been happier in life, always talking about someone bigger than himself. Not to blaspheme, but it seemed to him the harder job was having to be the biggest man in the here and now, not sitting up in the sky looking down and passing judgment. One day he'd have to account for himself at the pearly gates, maybe tonight, even, and justify each life he'd taken, right or wrong. He reckoned he got it right each time, but a man couldn't be sure; often didn't have the time to be sure. In that respect, the reverend had it easy, his job all written down in black and white. But even if Jed wasn't lily white, he was just righteous enough. Tonight would prove that, if nothing else.

The vampires were out there; he felt it. They were being cagey, encircling them and sticking to the deep shadows. Every so often, a boot scraping across the ground or a bush twitching in the still air would spook someone inside, reminding Jed he'd have to keep as close an eye inside as out.

"Why ain't they coming closer?" someone asked across the room. Man named Jake, if Jed remembered correctly. Wandering ranch hand and usually reliable, but also excitable. Jake had worked for John one season, and Jed supposed the man was lucky he was only a middling cowboy or he'd have been at John's…

No. He wasn't going to think about that now.

Cal put an arm on Jake's shoulder and tapped a finger to his own brow.

"They're playin' games with your head, Jake."

"Maybe they're planning on burning us out," a woman said, one of a trio everyone called the Lady Jays. Tough old spinsters who ran a small operation and also supplied Buzby with the occasional beer barrel. Jed remembered they were rightly called Fiona, Bea, and Danielle, but couldn't match up names with faces.

Jed said, "No need to borrow a cup of worry. If they want to wait out there, that's fine with me."

"You mean they're gonna starve us out?" she asked. She shared a look with one of the other Jays.

Cal strode over with an easy grin. "That's not the Apache way. They only have until sunup or else they gotta let us go."

"How you know that?" the other Jay said.

Cal shrugged. "I lived with a blind Apache when I was younger. Helped around the homestead, told stories and the like."

"Bullshit," said a man in the corner. Buzby had called him Hooper.

Cal grinned. "You'd like to think so. Tell you what, come sunup, I'll be the first one out the door, and if an

Apache scalps me, you can be the first one to say, 'I told you so.' Sound good?"

"You heard him, Sheriff!" Hooper said, and the Jays all cackled along.

"I did, and I'll hold him to it," Jed replied. He didn't know how Cal did it, walking around and getting half a dozen strangers to laugh and swear with him. For all the good it would do them. Cal might have a blessed bullet or two left in his pistols. Jed only had a half dozen himself, all loaded into the Peacemaker on his left. The right Starr held only the normal man-killing variety as did everyone else's, and the defenders would soon learn their paltry effect. Cal fixed this by partially tearing the stable apart and sharpening poles like spears, giving one to each man and the Jays with a reminder to stab for the heart. Jed reached out for his own spear, just to remind himself it was there. He thought about the other stake in his saddle bag and whether he should go get them. He wondered—

Figures skittered in from the dark.

Footsteps on the roof, scrabbling with boot scuff and long nails snapping cedar shakes.

"Get ready," he said

One of the Lady Jays brought her shotgun up as if she were going to take a shot through the roof. "Hold," Cal said. "Wait until you can see him."

"Watch the windows," Jed said.

More footsteps outside.

Jed moved over to Reverend Ellis and placed himself between the preacher and the open window. He looked out, but couldn't see shit. Jed kept looking into the dark, rubbing a clammy palm on his thigh. He looked away just as he caught a flash of movement, leaving the impression a thing that looked like a man but moved on all fours. In the back, a pistol cocked.

Then someone screamed, and Jed whirled around. Long knobby-knuckled hands burst through the wall, blowing bits of sod and dirt into the air. The taloned fingers tore into the man's chest, pulling him back as if trying to take him through the wall itself.

Cal was already running over, sticking his gun to the monster's wrist and firing. The hand spasmed open and Jed pulled the man back. Then Jake was there with his sharpened spear and jammed it through the hole, only to have the wood pulled through from the other side. Another set of hands burst from the other wall, next to one of the Jays. She screamed and backed away, eyes bulging at the taloned fingers swiping at the air. She brought her shotgun up and a swiping arm disappeared as she fired both barrels.

Jed kept one hand on Graham's chest and kept his gun ready. He needed a clear target.

Wood screeched overhead, nails popped, and a form fell from the ceiling. The vampire rose up from the dust, eyes red and teeth gleaming. Buzby unloaded his pistol into the thing, who danced and jerked backwards with each hit but didn't go down. Jed took aim.

Cal came up behind the vampire and slammed the stake through the man's back, its tip emerging out through his chest. The glowing eyes dimmed, and the vampire fell.

"That sure as hell don't look like an Indian to me," Jake said.

Cal shrugged and said, "You know, Jake, you might be right. I stand corrected."

A horse whinnied and reared in the stable, slamming its hooves into the side of its stall before falling over, dead. A red-eyed Crow with a bloody grin scrambled and ducked underneath the stable gate. The vampire continued through the bar and rushed on all fours at Cal's unprotected back.

Jed lowered his pistol and fired. The vampire jerked and stumbled aside but kept coming. Jed swore and went for the Peacemaker on his left side. He kept the draw smooth and the .45 took the vampire in the throat, and this time knocked it down. Buzby rushed in and put his substantial weight behind a spear to the thing's chest but missed his heart by a good bit. Buzby tried pulling his spear back, but he had driven the tip too deep into the floorboards.

Another scream to his left, and for a moment Jed thought one of the monsters had gotten to Reverend Graham. Instead, the vampire had wriggled through the side wall to its hips, its dirt-coated arms wrapped around Hooper, and fangs plunged into the side of the man's neck. Red eyes, without any hint of intelligence, stared at him like a rabid animal as Hooper's lifeblood dribbled from the corner of his lips. Jed lined up his shot, noting the flickers of intelligence starting to fill the vampire's eyes, an animal cunning replaced with mannish thoughts and intentions. The monster's wits recognized its danger a split second before Jed fired. It jerked Hooper's body into the bullet's path and pulled itself out from the wall. One of the other Jays was there to catch Hooper as he fell. She pulled him back and tried pressing a handkerchief to the man's ruined neck, but Jed knew Hooper was already dead.

Jed shouted, "Away from the walls!" He grabbed the reverend and pulled him farther in, and soon the remainder of the trading post were standing back-to-back, giving the pinned vampire on the floor a wide berth. They stayed that way for a goodly while, surrounded by the gunpowder's stench and haze before they realized the attack was over. Four bodies lay unmoving on Buzby's floor.

"Danielle!" Fiona Jay cried and rushed to the corner.

She turned a body over and froze. Beatrice handed her shotgun to Jake and strode over to embrace Fiona and turn her away from her dead companion. The spell broken, the others fanned out and began checking the other bodies. Judging from the blood on the walls and floor, Jed didn't believe any had survived their wounds.

"Well hello, there, Rory," Cal said to the vampire pinned to the floor. He called over to Jed. "Want me to finish him off?"

A plan formed in his head. "No. Take it outside and make sure it's chained to something damn heavy."

Chapter Twenty-Three

CAL LOOKED DOWN AT CREEPING RORY IN THE FALSE dawn's glow reflecting blues and purples off the surrounding hills and clouds shouldering in from the west. The former Crow was chained to an anvil, which in turn was bolted to the back of a broken-down wagon out back behind the trading post.

"You've looked better, Rory," Cal said. Rory glared up at him and his jaw unhinged like snake's before snapping at the air between them with a clack. Cal didn't know Rory all that well, though the man had always been a bit of a bootlicker. He supposed with Crazy Eye laid out in the dirt, Braga's coming had provided Rory with a new opportunity to toady up.

"I've got a question, Rory. Why didn't you try using a gun?" Cal asked.

Rory held up his manacled hands and the knobby, talon-tipped fingers grown to monstrous size. "It's a little hard getting these things around a trigger guard, ain't it? Besides, until your first feeding, all you can do is think about tearing flesh and guzzling your first hot, salty meal."

"Let me guess, you're regretting your decision?"

Rory looked over his shoulder at Buzby's ruined roof and walls as Jed emerged, heading their way. "Ain't gonna dwell on it, but yeah. Charging into a room full of guns isn't smart. Might have done it differently had I been thinking straight. Reason don't come back until you've fed. More's the pity." Rory looked up at Cal and said, "Don't worry, Trigger. Next time we meet, I'll be sure to bring a Winchester."

Jed stopped outside the chain's reach and looked down on Rory. "If we let you go, that is."

The tip of Rory's tongue darted out to the points of his fangs, rattlesnake quick. "Well, Sheriff, you could kill me. But if you do, you won't know what Lord Braga is planning."

Jed said, "There can't be that many more of you left or places worth hiding. I reckon we can track you down and smoke you out."

Rory laughed and yanked at his chains, making the wagon lurch. "We were the last of the hungry, Sheriff. You've been lucky up until now, but with the wilding gone, I expect you and Trigger here are gonna find yourselves facing a tougher bunch of *hombres*. If you want my advice, the smart play is to let me take a message to Lord Braga and iron out a settlement."

Jed noted the wagon's new position and backed up exactly that amount. "You'll forgive me if I let old judgments cloud my willingness to take you at your word and let you go, hoping for the best. The sun's about to come up, Rory, and based on what happened to Bryan Carter, I expect that'll go poorly for you. The smart play is you telling us where Braga's holed up, and we all go see what's what."

Cal didn't know so much about appealing to Rory's smarts, but he kept his face stoney.

Creeping Rory rattled his chain. "I'm going to need some reassurances before I tell you anything."

Jed tilted his hat back and scratched as he scalp as he let his gaze drift to the hills. He held out a thumb at arm's length and closed an eye, measuring the horizon's glow. "Well, Rory, you have my promise that if you tell us where Braga and Pete Williams are, we'll keep you under cover and out of the sun as a show of goodwill. If Braga promises to leave the valley and not bother us, reckon you can make your way down to Mexico with him, find yourself a new life to live, so to speak."

Rory looked at Trigger and said, "Can I trust him?"

Cal said, "He's been shooting straight with me so far." Then Cal looked at the horizon himself, the coming end of false dawn. "Besides, you dither too long, the sun's going to take care of your doubts for good."

Rory glanced over his shoulder and licked his lips before nodding. "Well, it's like this. Lord Braga, Pete Wilson, and what's left of the Crows, are all holed up at the old Dexter mine. I promise that if you let me go, I'll take a runner down Mexico way. That good enough, Sheriff?" He gave the coming light another glance and yanked at his chains.

Jed said, "Let me confer with my assistant here," and he motioned Cal to follow, well away from the wagon.

"What do you think?"

Cal said, "Never been out to the mine, but if you're afraid of the daylight, it's not a bad place to hide out. Lots of nooks and crannies, pure darkness."

"Only a day's ride from there to Sunset."

Cal said, "Yeah, a little closer than it's probably comfortable. I also don't know if we can trust Rory, but I suppose the sun will keep him pinned until we get back, provided we round up a heavy blanket for him to crawl under."

Jed said, "Doesn't seem to me that matters much."

Cal turned to him, puzzled. "I don't take your meaning."

Jed said, "A man's word is between himself and another man. From where I stand, that thing chained to the anvil ain't no man, nothing more than a talking dog. One that's responsible for killing three men plus a woman. That's a dog you put down."

Creeping Rory leapt to his feet, jerked at his chains, which rattled and hummed as the anvil strained at the wagon's bolts. "You gave your word, Sheriff."

Jed called out, "Some mighty sharp ears that you've got there. I apologize for speaking where you could still hear me. It was unkind."

"So you're going to keep me chained up here for the rest of time?"

Jed looked at the horizon and said, "Not nearly that long. You go ahead and make your peace with your maker. Better talk fast and speak sweetly, though. From what I understand, your soul's already been condemned."

Rory spat between them and heaved against the chains, rocking the old wagon a good three inches before he gave up and sat on the ground. "When I see the devil, I'll tell him to save a spot for you, right next to me. We're going to be *good* friends, Jedidiah Scott. Good friends!"

Jed shrugged. "You be careful what you wish for, Rory. If we end up in the same place in the hereafter, the devil is going to be the least of your problems."

True dawn crested over the hills and set Rory's skin blistering as he covered his face with overlarge, knobby hands.

"I told you what you wanted!"

Jed considered the words, head tilted. "You know what, Rory? You're right. You want a blanket over you or something?"

"Yes!"

"Here's why I'm not going to do that," Jed said. "Remember two years back? You and Crazy Eye's little visit outside Santa Fe? Old fella by the name of Clark Barker?"

"Wasn't our fault. He drew first!"

Jed nodded slowly. "So you do remember him. Except the way I heard it, you jumped him in the night."

"The hell we did." Rory hissed and flattened himself against the ground, trying to hide in the last of the night's shadows. "Just lies from the marshal on account of Clark being his drinking buddy."

Jed went to a knee and leaned over Rory's smoldering form. "Not just the marshal's. Clark taught all us in the territory how to be lawmen. He earned a longer retirement, Rory, deserved better than getting knifed in the back by two low-lifes."

"The hell we did."

The sun broke over the hills and Rory screamed as his flesh bubbled and blackened. Rory lifted his face to Jed and snarled.

"You're a cursed man! Oath breaker!" Rory's eyes bulged. Fluid popped and sizzled down his face. He turned empty sockets on Cal. "You too, Trigger."

Cal's heart seized as icy fingers gripped it. For a moment it seemed it would stop altogether, but the fingers relaxed as Rory thumped to the ground and his body turned to ash. The chill lingered and felt like it would never warm again.

Jed poked at the ashes with a stick, moving the empty

manacles aside. "Not a lot left to 'em in the end." He glanced over his shoulder with a grin, which faded as he studied Cal.

Jed's head tilted, puzzled. "You don't believe him, the curse?"

Cal shook his head. "I don't," but he couldn't figure out how to make Jed understand without making himself look like a yellow-bellied fool. "Made me feel cold all over is all," he managed.

"I don't believe in curses, Calvin, and neither should you."

Cal toed the empty manacles and spat the sourness from his mouth. "You think so, Jedidiah? Up until a few days ago, you didn't believe in vampires either."

Chapter Twenty-Four

JAKE CAME RUNNING OUT OF BUZBY'S AND TOOK PAUSE AT the man-shaped ash pile. "That…?"

The man had a strange mix of fear and curiosity warring across his face. Jed remembered feeling something similar the morning after a battle, when they'd been detailed to see after the dead. He'd remembered feeling lucky to still be alive while also gaping over the myriad ways he could have died. "What's left of Creeping Rory," he said.

"Right." Jake shook himself. "Reverend Graham is coming 'round."

"Now Jake, these things don't like sunlight," Jed said. "So they go to ground during the day."

"Likely at the Dexter mine," Cal said.

Jake nodded. "Right at the end of Beggar's Canyon, good place if you hate the sun. There's all the darkness a man or beast could want."

"You know it?" Jed asked.

Jake shrugged and began poking at Rory's ashes with Jed's stick. "Worked there until the silver started running out. I was one of the lucky ones that quit it early. That place was a widow maker."

"Even more a death trap now," Cal said. Jed followed the man's gaze as Buzby and his customers emerged, including the remaining Lady Jays, trailing with their heads together.

Jed recalled stories about the mine, but it hadn't seemed any more dangerous than others. "Widow maker how?" he asked.

Jake spat onto the ashes. "The seams are crisscrossed with a disagreeable mix of granite and quartz that loves to fragment. A real corker to tunnel through. We had to use picks most times because dynamite would more often than not bring a tunnel down around your ears. But even then, we had accidents."

"So if someone happened to toss a few sticks in the front door?" Jed said.

Jake shook his head. "If you're fixing to bury some folk and make sure it took, you'd want to blow the supports."

"Sounds like you know exactly how to go about it," Jed said.

Jake paused and looked between Jed and Cal, then pointed at the ash pile. "Look, I ain't going into a nest of those things."

"Would you rather let them fester?" Cal said.

"I don't like the idea any more than you do, Jake, but every day we let these things have their way will be that much harder for us to root 'em out." He turned and addressed the others, catching a few eyeing their horses and rickety wagons parked among the scattered wrecks. "I need all of you to come along and see this through."

The others kept silent, shooting looks back and forth until Fiona stepped forward. "One of them killed my sister. I'm in."

Bea pulled at Fiona's arm. "No! I'm not losing both of you."

Fiona shook her arm free. "Go back to the ranch, Bea."

Jed looked to Buzby, who held up his hands. "I can give you a box of dynamite and a blasting box, but…" He grabbed his round belly with both hands and shook it. "I'm no good in a fight, Sheriff. Besides, who's gonna watch the post if I'm gone?"

Jed looked to the others, who wouldn't meet his eyes. Some people are sheep, some are wolves, and the sheep had always outnumbered men like him. Maybe Cal and Fiona would be enough, but he doubted it. Hopefully Sarah would forgive him breaking his vow.

From Buzby's entrance, a voice rattled, gaining strength and timbre with every word. "Brothers and sisters! Are we forgetting the lessons of Jeremiah? 'They will stumble repeatedly; they will fall over each other. They will say, "Get up, let us go back to our own people and our native lands, away from the sword of the oppressor." And as surely as the people of Egypt, we too will fall like sheaves of wheat to the scythe if we do not stand.'" A pale and sweating Reverend Graham pushed away from the doorway and pressed a hand to his severed stump. "I will go, brothers and sisters, even as I am, with my resolve undiminished. Can you do no less?"

Those with downcast eyes shifted and their faces flushed. Jed was about to tell the reverend to go back inside and lie down when Buzby took a step forward.

"I'll go," he said and went to stand by Cal and Fiona.

The others followed suit, except Bea, who simply turned on her heel and went inside.

Jed nodded to Graham and looked to the group around him. "Grab your guns and mount up." He nodded to the bank of clouds coming in from the northwest. "There's a storm coming, and I want to catch them while we still have full daylight."

As the group broke up, Jed went to Graham and leaned in so the others wouldn't hear. The stench of blood, burnt flesh, and iron yet clung to him, but it didn't seem to bother the preacher any.

"I don't mean to cross your Bible knowledge, Reverend, but I don't recall that part of Jeremiah going the way you mean," Jed said.

Graham wiped his brow and gave him a baleful look. "I find the Good Book is ever lending itself to cutting through the confusion plaguing a man's mind if presented correctly. If we rid the Earth of these abominations, I'm willing to believe the good Lord will overlook my lapse in nuance. Now if that will be all, Jedidiah, kindly help get me on my damn mule."

Chapter Twenty-Five

CAL HADN'T PAID ANY PARTICULAR ATTENTION TO THE Dexter Mine on account of there being nothing worth stealing. The rust-weeping tailing mounds, rainbow-colored pools, and sickly yellow scrub along the meandering trail only reinforced his opinion. No birds sang in Beggar's Canyon, no critters scattered at their approach, only the biting black flies kept them company as the posse's hoofbeats echoed from the narrowing walls.

Jed had placed himself up front and kept looking over his shoulder at the roiling clouds. They had run the horses harder than Cal would have liked, but to keep the sun, they needed to push their mounts. Sacrificing horse flesh might just save their own.

Graying timbers framed the Dexter's tunnel entrance, sunlight penetrating only a few feet into the inky darkness beyond. The mine's head frame, a 30-foot tower of criss-crossed rusting metal topped by a spoked wheel, held taut a brown-stained cable disappearing into the hillside. Cal didn't exactly like the look of it, but Jake assured him that the elevator attached to the cable's end would support three men. They tied the horses off against the old mill works, Cal careful to keep their thirsty horses well away from any standing and surely poisoned water.

Jed quickly organized them into groups, each with a lantern, a bundle of dynamite, and a wire reel. As they entered the tunnels, Cal's relief in the cooler air was tempered by the feeble lanterns' light barely cutting through the darkness and making their shadows all jumpy and jerking. Cal wasn't happy with his ration from Buzby's lantern oil either, and suspected the drizzle would run out exactly when he needed it most. It set his brain and fingers itching to hold a Navy's reassuring weight in his hand as they pushed farther into the dark.

But mostly Cal was worried about the silence and how it held as thick as mud in his ears in the moments between boot steps and quickened breaths. As the others peeled away with their bundles of dynamite, Cal's eyes kept picking out flickers at the edge of the lantern's light, wondering if it was a vampire ready to leap. His hand went to his chest pocket and twisted the calico between his fingers.

"Where do you reckon they are?" Cal asked Jed. "If it were me, I would have posted guards at the entrance. Spotters. But I didn't hear nothing. I don't see nothing."

Jed nodded. "Not even boot prints in the dirt."

Cal looked to the walls. "Assuming they step on the floor like men anymore. Could be they climb the walls or the ceilings, like spiders."

Jed said, "You are just a bundle of optimism and hope."

Jake left the others to place charges along support beams and took Jed and Cal around a bend to the elevator shaft. The elevator itself was little more than a metal cage with a splintered wood floor and thin chains at waist-level for railings. A smear of sunlight shone overhead where the cable entered the top of the shaft, clouds tempering the light to a wan circle at their feet

Jake took up a rusty winch's hand crank. "They took the engine out when they closed the place down, but you can work the wheel by hand," he explained. Jake demonstrated its operation and Cal and Jed joined him sending the cage down. "The main gallery is down one level."

"And that's the key to taking this place down?" Jed asked.

"The mine's first owners got too greedy digging out the gallery, so the second group had to shore it up with steel scaffolds, which put them in the red. The last owners were always worried that the slightest tremor from an errant blast or some drunk miner running an ore cart into the beams would bring the whole thing collapsing down," Jake said. "Didn't stop anything, mind, but they were worried."

"Hell of an operation," Cal muttered.

Jake shrugged. "It made money, after a fashion."

The winch squeaked, and their struggling sent the cage knocking against the shaft's sides, echoing loud in Cal's ears. He couldn't help but think he was ringing his own death knell and said as much.

"Maybe they're not here," Jake said.

Jed said, "If not, we'll deny them a refuge to stay. But you can feel it, can't you?" he asked Cal.

The ache in Cal's shoulder throbbed, and he tasted copper at the back of mouth. He nodded. "It certainly don't feel empty."

Jake tied off the elevator as it came to the next level, unhooking a chain and stepping through. Cal tried not to think of the tons of rock overhead and the chances of one of the others up top sneezing or otherwise setting off their charge early and burying him here forever. So he kept his eyes forward, gun at the ready, and worked to keep his boots from echoing in the tunnel.

The passage opened up into a chamber whose walls and ceiling the lanterns' glow barely touched. Jed swore softly and pointed. Cal's head swiveled and he found seven figures high up on the walls, clinging to the rock like bats. He recognized Pete right away next to a larger, darker shape with the oily skin that had to be Lord Braga. A few other Dust Crows were also there. The vampires' eyes were closed, and their breaths came quickly as if they were hyperventilating or starved for breath.

"Reckon they're sleeping?" Jed whispered.

Cal nodded, then reached out to push Jake's lantern slowly to the floor and put the sleeping monsters back into shadow. "That's what we got to stop, Jake. We're counting on you. If they get out, it could be the end of not just us, but all of the valley and more."

"I got it, Sheriff," Jake whispered.

Jed pulled Jake by his shoulder. "Whatever it takes."

Jake nodded once. "Whatever it takes."

"Lead on," he said, pointing his chin into the darkness.

Jake's pale face turned away, and with hunched shoulders led them to a series of steel pillars that ran from floor to ceiling.

Cal leaned in and whispered, "You know, I reckon with them sleeping, I could take half the vampires on my own, you take the other half, and we finish this right now. We have enough of the Reverend's bullets that we could down 'em like pigeons before they woke up and knew what was what."

Jed shook his head. "We stick to the plan. It's too risky if we miss, then we're caught down here with them all around us."

Cal thought the man was wasting a gift, but he knew

he couldn't take all the vampires out without the sheriff's help. "But we could end it here."

"I mean to get us all out alive, Trigger. After that, you can do as you please."

"I'll hold you to that," Cal said. He took a bundle of dynamite from Jake and placed it at the base of the pillar, sticking in the primers the way Jake had shown them. They soon got the job done and spooled the wire back to the elevator, each keeping one eye on the wire, the other on the sleeping vampires above.

Cal got one last look at Pete, not resting peacefully at all, huffing like he was in a fever, eyes bulging behind pale lids. A cruel frown on him, even in sleep. Pete used to not be such a bad guy, as Cal remembered. Always sly and on the lookout for the best deal for himself first and his brother second, but nowhere near the worst scoundrel Cal had known. Somewhere along the way, Pete had grown mean, and Cal couldn't quite place where it happened. Not that Cal could throw too many stones himself, but at least he was here on the side of the living and not crawling behind the beast that had killed his friends.

Maybe Jed had the right of it, not taking the fight to the vampires. Probably because he had a wife and kids. Maybe if things with Jenny had gone different, he wouldn't have suggested the reckless plan either. His hand went to his pocket, and he promised himself this was it: he would be going to San Francisco on the next train out.

As they reached the elevator, the smear of overhead sunshine faded. Then the shaft lit up, leaving Cal blinking away purple blotches as thunder rumbled. Cal put his hands on the winch but stopped at Jed's gesture. Jed cocked his head, then Cal heard it, too. A scrape of leather against stone, a fluttering of cloth, then a series of an indrawn series of breaths from the chamber beyond. Muffled thumps, like men dropping from great heights.

Jed brought up the lantern and dim eyes reflected pink light back to him from the darkness.

"Sweet Jesus," Jake whispered.

They started hauling on the elevator winch, as fast as they could. They drove hand over hand, the elevator crawling upwards as footsteps thundered. The platform lurched sideways and clanged against stone. Through the slats at Cal's feet, red eyes gleamed. Pale claws dug into the wood under his boots and pulled a board partially free.

Jed pulled his Starr and fired through the slats, making the vampires hiss and sending the elevator swinging. The three of them hauled at the winch, its squeaking becoming a screeching. Cal shouted ahead of them, warning the others to get out even as the burn of working the winch set into his arms. Jed fired again, but from another quarter, claws grabbed at Cal's boot and held on like it was nailed to the elevator's floor. The burning in Cal's arms doubled and the blood pounded in his ears as he strained just to keep the platform from dropping. He felt the creatures latch on underneath the platform like ticks, and the winch gears strained until one slipped three teeth, sending them all dropping with metal sparking against granite.

Another tug, and Cal had to ease the winch back another inch or risk stripping out the contraption's gears entirely. His boot heel, proof against dozens of rattlesnake bites, collapsed as the vampire's talons worked through and scraped against his skin.

Jed drew his Peacemaker and fired blindly, to the left and right, ricochets loud in the shaft, deafening Cal's ears. The last shot found the right angle, eliciting a grunt from underneath. The weight from his foot lifted, and the elevator cage shot up the shaft as snarls and gibbering echoed from below.

The three cranked for what seemed like eternity but was likely only a few seconds before Jake pushed them out and fidgeted with the winch. He leapt backwards as the assembly let loose from the cable and tumbled down the shaft.

Cal didn't know what he shouted, only that the others took notice and rushed for the mine entrance. Cal noted the first patters of rain on his face as he turned and pulled his guns while Jake rushed past with the fuse wires.

Lightning flashed, illuminating the vampires boiling out of the elevator shaft like spiders from a hole. Cal and the others opened up with a hail of bullets that took the two in the lead, but it barely slowed them down while others scrambled behind it along the walls and ceiling. A vampire screamed as it left the shadows, skin blistering even under the cloudy sky. Cal squeezed off a shot at it but missed as a force shook his mind and set his raked shoulder ablaze with pain. Braga's voice whispered in his head, and Cal shook to clear it.

Are you ready, Calvin Jones?

Another vampire leapt at Cal and he fired, taking it in the shoulder, but it kept coming. He fired twice more, in the chest and face, before it fell. He swung the gun around to cover Fiona, but her attacker tumbled into her before he could clear a shot. Cal had only taken a single step when the vampire rolled into a ball and gained his feet, dashing back with the screaming Fiona held overhead, into the mine's darkness. Reverend Graham went after her, and Cal followed, catching up just inside the mine's entrance, and hauling him back.

"It's a trap, Reverend!"

"Let me go, boy!" He tried shaking Cal off, but the man's sapped strength couldn't overcome Cal's.

Jed and Buzby were holding the flanks, firing with pistols in one hand, and waving cedar stakes in the other. Cal pulled Graham back into the rain and fell to the ground as someone caught him from his blind side. Pete knocked him to the ground with a strength of a buffalo.

"Hello, Trigger."

Cal scrambled to his feet and tried backing into the full light, but Pete clamped onto Cal's calf and pulled. Cal fell to his back and twisted away, wrenching his foot from Pete's grip. He went for his pistol, but Pete pinned his arm and leaned in with bared fangs.

Cal got a hand on Pete's forehead and pushed.

Pete snarled, caught Cal's wrist and squeezed, sending pain shooting up his arm as bones crunched together. Pete's breath blew cold across his neck as the jaws descended.

His thumb worked around Pete's chin and hooked under the jawbone.

A tooth scraped across his skin, drawing blood.

Then Graham was there, voice booming, and Pete's strength flagged under the reverend's litany. Cal shoved Pete's head away and flipped his hips, sending them both tumbling. He came up on top with a forearm across Pete's throat. Pete raked at him with his nails, but Cal ducked his head to escape the worst of it and worked his backup Patterson free from its holster.

He brought it to Pete's chest and fired twice. Pete twitched but kept fighting, pushing the gun's barrel away from his heart.

Graham's litany stuttered as a chill blast blew from the mine's depths. Cal's eyes were drawn deeper into the tunnel where Jed had driven a cedar stake through a Dust

Crow's chest, splintering it. Jed's hand bled some, but the vampire got the worst of it with skin turning ashen and withering.

Then a tall shadow rose behind Jed, an oil-slicked void that made Cal's heart freeze. A pale arm flashed out and Jed staggered back with his chest torn to ribbons. Braga emerged, his moldering robes replaced with modern duds, complete with hat and a long duster, emaciated flesh replaced with ropy muscle on a tall frame that stood with a swordsman's grace. Braga's ruby eyes gleamed as they took in Jed's shredded skin and muscle before turning to Cal.

"It is time to join me," Braga said in a deep voice that resonated through Cal's bones. "My brand already etches your mortal flesh." Braga pressed a taloned finger to his shoulder and Cal felt the poke echoed in his own.

Cal looped an arm around Pete's neck and hauled him up. He held the gun to Pete's ear as he walked, keeping Pete between himself and Braga, forcing the ancient monster away from Jed and back towards elevator's ruin. "Back off."

Braga tilted his head. "I think not. Your blood runs hot, not cold."

Pete sucked in a pained breath. "He'll do it, Lord."

"Let us see," Braga said.

"What?" Pete said. Then to Cal, "This how it gonna end between us, Cal?"

"You always were the quickest when it came to saving your own skin," Cal said.

"At least make it a fair fight," Pete said.

"We had it already. You lost," Cal said and tensed.

"Wait—"

Cal shifted his aim and fired, taking Braga in the chest. He holstered the Patterson and brought up a stake with his other hand. While Pete still hadn't realized he'd not been shot, his body was already moving when Cal drove the stake through his back.

Cal pushed Pete into the reeling Braga, then slammed a shoulder into the pair, sending them tumbling down the shaft. Cal spun on his heel and hastened to Jed, putting a shoulder under the sheriff and hauling the man to his feet. He turned them towards the light. Graham's one-armed silhouette wavered ahead of them and the preacher shouted something that Cal couldn't make out. Graham pointed, and in the lee of the millworks, Jake had the detonator wired in and plunger raised.

"Let's get a hurry on, Jed," Cal said. The lawman grunted and they stumbled along a little faster. Graham joined them and added his strength to Cal's.

Buzby picked himself up from the floor, holding his arm at a strange angle.

"You too, Buzby!" Cal shouted.

A chill blew across Cal's neck and Jake's eyes grew large.

The plunger fell.

The blast picked them up in mid-step, sending them flying. Dust and rock rained down, and the only thought in Cal's mind was to keep his legs moving, no matter what. Darkness and confusion closed around him except for a smudge of gray he headed for, pulling Jed along with him. Cal felt an itch between his shoulder blades, one that would turn to a searing line when Braga's talons caught up to him. That is, if the falling rocks around them didn't split his skull like an overripe melon.

Cal slipped and fell into the light, Jed crying out beside him. A shock ran through his arms and rusty mud filled his mouth, but he was still in one piece. Jed was sprawled on his back, as was Graham beyond them.

Alive. He was alive.

The mine's entrance was gone, replaced by a tumble of boulders and rubble. The head frame's spoked wheel and tower lay toppled as well, sticking out of a depression where the elevator shaft entrance had been.

Jake ran up with glee on his face. "We got 'em! We sure got 'em!"

The ground rumbled beneath them like a man working through a bad meal. Deep percussive snaps and aftershocks rumbled, then silence. Moments later, a weak call, unintelligible.

"Where's Buzby?" Jed said. Cal shook his head.

"Why didn't you wait?" Jed shouted. His fist started curling.

"That thing was right behind you, Sheriff! You said…"

"You did good, Jake," Cal interrupted and looked right at Jed. "You followed orders. We all would have died if you hadn't."

Jed looked back at the mine's remains, then down at the gouges in his chest. "Reckon so. Apologies, Jake."

Jake went still as he looked past Cal and realized who the call was coming from. "We'll dig him out," he said.

"With what? Hands? Camp shovels?" Jed said, a little harsher than Cal thought fair. "He's gone, Jake, and it's not on you, it's on me." He stumbled, and Cal caught him in both arms.

"You wanna help, Jake? Get some bandages and thread," Cal said, sending Jake off at a sprint for the horses while Cal set the sheriff down.

Jed looked down at his bloody chest and picked at the remains of his shirt. "Mrs. Scott won't appreciate me having ruined this. Don't expect she'll be able to sew it back together, neither."

"She'd appreciate digging a six-foot hole for your pine box less," Cal said.

Jed smiled. "I expect so."

Jake came back with the supplies and Cal took up the needle and thread, seeing as Jake was getting the shakes and Graham only having the one arm. He got Jed settled and went to work sewing him up. Jed winced but didn't flinch from what Cal knew was about as pleasant as rolling around in a fire ant nest.

Cal tried distracting the wounded man, saying, "I know it's not the way you wanted it, but that's the last you'll see of Braga, Pete, and the Crows. Reckon I'm out of the game, too. Soon enough you'll have the trains coming back, and the most you'll have to worry about is the odd drunk or fella selling miracle cures out of a carpet bag."

"A quiet life," Jed said. "They make those for men like us?"

"I aim to find out," Cal said and tied off the string. *And this time I really mean it, Jenny.*

Chapter Twenty-Six

THE AFTERNOON'S CLOUDBURST PASSED QUICKLY, LINGERING long enough to foul the trail yet providing the land no relief. The cooler air soon turned muggy and miserable as the clouds blew east and the sun resumed in full force, quickly drying out the mud on the trail and baking it onto the hooves of the horses and steaming the men within their dusters and jackets. Cal took his duster off and laid it across the saddle, spreading it to try to dry it some. His shoulder's bandages were soaked through and sticky with blood, but Jed's bindings had been more important than changing his own. He reckoned they would make Sunset long before he had to worry about things going septic.

Reverend Graham slept in the saddle with Jake riding beside him, the former miner there to make sure the reverend didn't fall over. Jake kept a patter going all the way from the mine, trying to keep the men both awake and upbeat.

Cal's relief from surviving the fight gave over to irritation. Jake was one of those men who was perpetually happy, and he couldn't just sit and let a man wallow in his own misery and work things out on his own. He kept it swallowed for a goodly while, but after the hundredth exclamation about the beauty of the distant mountains, Cal told Jake it would be best for his health if he shut his jaw for a spell and focused on keeping Graham in his saddle. Jake looked to Jed for a differing opinion, but the sheriff said nothing and stared down the trail, letting Cactus pick his own path.

The pace, slow on account of the abused horses, meant that what little sunlight remained in the day disappeared by the time they hit the outskirts of town. Cal appreciated not having to look back over his shoulder as darkness fell, although he caught himself doing just that every time his shoulder throbbed. He still saw the vampires when he closed his eyes, his mind imagining taloned hands shifting through rubble as bodies driven mad with pain plotted revenge. He hoped it would disappear in the coming days and not linger, like the musket ball he had taken to his calf years ago at a skirmish that hadn't merited a name. It still twinged at odd times, the muscle that never quite regained its wholeness and always reminded him of gunpowder and a pink-stained creek when it twinged. He didn't want to think about the memories his shoulder would conjure, and with enough whiskey, he reckoned he wouldn't have to.

He wondered if nightmares stuck to Jed. The man had lost more than a bit of blood, taken a shock, and damn near got buried today, but he sat in the saddle like it was the parade ground. Hell, he had probably been born that way. But the man was hurting: the little signs showing around his eyes, a stiffness to the way he handled Cactus, and the hitch in his breath when the horse stumbled over a loose rock. He wanted to ask, but he gave the sheriff his space.

Cal figured he wasn't too different from Jed. They had

both seen the war, they had both come out to the territory to remake themselves. It was just a flip of life's coin that Jed would end up on one side of the law and Cal the other. Perhaps the world needed men like Cal so Jed and his kind could stay in business as lawmen. Cal turned the idea over in his mind. Flip the coin. Might he become a lawman, too? Change his name, go into a new town? Once the people had gotten used to him, he could set about getting a badge. Not a marshal, not necessarily a sheriff with a stable of deputies, maybe just a tiny office in a small town. He imagined he could handle any trouble a village might get. Enough respectability to keep him straight, in a town out of the way enough to not tempt him with thieving.

But who was he kidding? If he were betting on himself, he wouldn't expect more than a month before it all went sideways. What he did know was he wouldn't be able to stay in Sunset Valley much longer. The Six were gone, and he reckoned he owed Jed a little too much to be carrying on within his territory. Better to go somewhere else and harass some other lawman, perhaps one that wasn't quite as quick with his guns.

When they reached Sunset, they had to weave their way past overturned wagons, barrels, sawhorses, and other odds and ends that had been thrown up at both ends of town. Sunset had done well in the past two days, putting up a formidable barrier that would have held off an entire cavalry company. Cal wanted to be a fly on the wall when Jed told Mayor Hornsby that everything was safe and the townsfolk could take it all down again. Cal also made a note to clear out before somebody started recruiting or press-ganging people like him for such a task.

Hornsby came out to greet them with a rifle in his hand. The mayor looked up expectantly at Jed, who just leaned down from his saddle and said, "The town can sleep easy tonight."

The mayor clasped Jed on the leg and started beaming. "That's capital, Sheriff, just capital! I'll go and tell the others."

The townsfolk, which had been manning the barricades and the roofs, had a wariness about them that evaporated with the news. As relief spread amongst them, a few even shook hands as they started coming down from rooftops. Cal could see why the mayor had been elected, as he was able to keep his lies straight while still reassuring everyone the danger had passed.

Cal said, "What now, Sheriff?"

Jed said, "First thing, I reckon we should head back to the jailhouse." There must have been a look on Cal's face that amused the sheriff, because he broke into a genuine smile and said, "Why don't you meet me at the saloon instead? I'll be along presently after I check in with Otto. Tell Sarah the first bottle's on me."

Cal allowed himself to relax. "I suppose I can manage that."

Cal had once thought the saloon was rather plain and modest, little more than a pine bar top, some tables, and a few bottles trying desperately to fill an entire shelf. In fact, the only advantage it held over Buzby's watering hole was that Jed's wife kept it clean, and had rooms upstairs for the sporting girls when they deigned to stop at Sunset before making their way to Yuma or Kansas City on the circuit.

Cal had generally preferred the saloons in Yuma and Kansas City himself and couldn't blame the women for cutting their stays short and moving on to fancier and more lucrative venues. Places where music and dancing could be had along with a wider selection of libations. Tonight, Cal appreciated the saloon's simplicity and quiet.

He appreciated the seven bottles on the shelf making his choices easier. He especially appreciated the lack of a sporting girl in residence, because he wasn't very good company and was broke besides.

Jed's wife looked up from the bar and then beyond over his shoulder. She smiled but held her arms stiff somewhat like she had a weapon hidden up her sleeve. She seemed to steel herself as he approached, and Cal waved a hand, putting on his second-best smile.

"The sheriff will be along shortly. Said he had to check on the deputy and such."

Mrs. Scott was handsome rather than pretty, blonde hair and fine dress's waist tightly bound with ribbons as befitting a woman of station. She relaxed and she gave him a polite smile that hinted at the beauty she must have been once upon a time, and probably could still polish up if she ever escaped a dusty town like Sunset.

"Did you take care of the ... bandits?" she asked.

"They won't bother us anymore, Mrs. Scott."

"Then how about a whiskey on the house?"

Cal laughed. "Jed said that he was buying, but it makes no difference to me, Mrs. Scott."

"Well, if the sheriff's office is buying." She grabbed a bottle and poured three glasses. "And it's Sarah, please, if we're going to be drinking together." They clinked glasses, and Cal savored the sweet burn all the way down. Sarah refilled his glass, though he noted her own was still half full.

"Jed said those creatures had to be put down," Sarah said.

"That they did."

"He also said they had stained souls that would never come clean."

Cal looked at his sorry self in the mirror behind the

bar and quickly looked away, taking another drink. "Might be. Reverend Graham thought otherwise."

She poured more whiskey. "What do you think?"

Cal studied his glass. Most of them had been beyond help. The problem would be picking the ones that could be saved from the others, which was a hell of a thing to do in a gun fight. "They were all damned, ma'am. Take it from a man who'd know."

Sarah set both hands on the bar and lowered her voice. "Was it bad?" she asked.

Cal paused with the lie on his lips, how it was nothing more troublesome than a lost steer, but he could still feel the talons ripping his flesh and see glowing red eyes in the darkness when he closed his eyes. He also, belatedly, realized she wasn't asking on his account but for Jed's, so he nodded. "Yeah. It was bad," and tossed the drink back. She paused for a moment before doing the same herself and refilling their glasses.

The saloon doors banged behind him, and Cal's hand dropped to his guns before he registered Jed's tall frame, fresh shirt, and an amused look on his face. Sarah put her glass down and ran to Jed, who set his feet wide to meet her embrace, lest he get tackled. Cal turned away, feeling as if he were seeing something he shouldn't, not because it was scandalous, but because of what it stirred up in his chest He patted the lump in his chest pocket and calmed himself down.

Sarah and Jed joined Cal at the bar, and she pushed the third glass to her husband. She glanced at Jed's chest. "Where's your badge?"

"Left it in the office and taking the evening off. You sampling your own stock?"

Sarah lifted a shoulder. "Heard the sheriff was buying and didn't think he'd mind if I joined in for just one." She glanced at Cal, daring him to say different. Cal gave her a half wink to let her know her secret was safe with him.

Jed shook his head. "Not at all, miss." He held up his glass. "To peace and order." They clinked glasses and drank.

Cal held up his glass. "To seeing another sunrise." They clinked glasses, and sweet fire spread from his belly into his limbs and fingertips. Sarah stepped back with her glass and excused herself. Cal reached for the bottle himself and tried to top off Jed's glass, but the sheriff waved him off. "The bottle's yours, Cal. Call it a reward if you like. You certainly earned it."

"Then you can't tell me who I can and can't share it with," Cal said with more heat than he intended.

Jed spun his glass in his hand, tapping its bottom on the bar top as he gave a grudging nod. "All right, Cal," he said quietly. "But not too much. I've still got to play sheriff come morning."

"Better you than me," Cal said.

"I'll drink to that."

And they did.

Chapter Twenty-Seven

THE LIGHT OUTSIDE WAS BURNING HIS EYES, BUT CAL screwed his courage to open one eyelid, sending a spear of lightning shooting through his head. His brain pulsed with aftershocks, and by the time it subsided, his other senses returned. It tasted like a buzzard had taken a dump right into his mouth, and something sour in the air curdled his stomach. His arm had fallen asleep under him, and when he rolled to the side, he barked his elbow on a hard brick wall. He peeled the eye open again, slowly, against the sunshine and tried to recollect what had happened. He remembered finishing the bottle with Jed, and that Jed had kindly bought him another one. Sarah had retired for the night, then they'd gone into the wee hours in the morning as they swapped war stories. What had happened after that?

Cal sat up and instantly regretted it. He hadn't gotten drunk like this in a goodly while and now remembered why. As his eyes adjusted to the light, he discovered that Jed had a sense of humor after all and had dumped him back in the jailhouse. He was back in his old bunk and noted he had also managed to vomit on the floor. He shimmied to the side, away from the mess, and put on his boots.

The room spun as he stood, and he put his hands on the cell bars as he steadied himself. When he recovered, he tugged at the bars, but the cell door wouldn't budge.

"Very funny, Jed," Cal said. "Get over here and let me out. I promise I'll clean up the mess."

No answer. Boots scraped across the floorboards in the office, then a door opened and closed.

"Come on, Jed, this isn't funny," Cal said.

It came to dawn on him as he stopped to listen that there wasn't anyone else in the jailhouse. He patted his sides and realized that his gun belt was missing, too. He slapped at his pocket and felt some scant relief that the calico lump was still there.

Cal craned his neck around the bars and sure enough, his guns were up on the office wall next to Jed's calvary sword. Something thumped in the cell next door. The vampire box was still there, as was its occupant, muttering and scratching at the insides. It wasn't right, that that thing being in the cell next to him. It was a joke gone too far.

Cal banged on the cell bars, shouted, swore, but to no avail. Cal jumped on top of his bunk and looked past the rust-spotted bars on the window. The townspeople outside were setting Sunset back to normal, some dismantling barricades and moving wagons off the street, while others pulled boards off of windows. A few grumbled about the whole operation already, wondering if there had even been a threat in the first place,

A few minutes later, the office door opened, closed, and Jed came walking into the cell block. If he was feeling poorly from wounds or drink, it didn't show. His eyes were bright, his jaw freshly shaved, his badge gleaming in the cell block's dim light. Cal jumped down and gripped the bars. "This isn't funny, Jed, I need you to let me out," he said.

Jed pulled up a chair and swung a leg over it to sit on it. "'Fraid I can't do that, Cal."

"I'm quite interested in knowing why," Cal said. "I was under the impression we were about to go our separate ways under friendly terms."

Jed readjusted his hat and said, "The Wild Six ran a job down in Arizona territory. Small town called Woodland."

Cal's heart lurched, and he smelled gun smoke. "I seem to recollect," he said.

Jed said, "Do you remember a body on the ground?"

She lay face-down, dark hair splayed like a wet mop, dark stains spreading across her new calico dress. Pete screaming at him wild-eyed. Cal said, "Vividly."

Jed said, "Well, that was Marshal Luke Rodgers."

Cal was thrown. Jed went on to explain about some fella that Jed had served with in the cavalry, went on to be a lawman after the war or some such. All Cal could think of was Jenny's body on the ground. Someone screaming that might have been him. Pete running around into the bank and out again, shooting the place up along with anyone who came running down the street. His icy clarity had left him in that moment, leaving him only with impressions of Jenny going limp. How heavy she'd been to pick up and how slippery his hands got. He didn't rightly recall anything coherent until he was already outside Woodland, Jenny across his saddle, swearing to her that she was going to be all right as soon as he found a doctor, but knowing deep down she was already dead.

"… the warrant is still active," Jed finished.

Cal asked Jed, "Were you there?"

Jed said that he was not. He'd read the reports, talked to a few men who'd been there.

Cal asked, "Was there anything said about another body on the ground?" Jed shook his head

"Funny, that. You'd think a lung shot woman would stick in someone's memory. Jenny, she was. Gonna get married one day, but she got caught in a crossfire. She was only supposed to be a lookout. Didn't have a gun. Wouldn't have gotten in a line of fire, but somebody with more swagger than sense shot wild, and it took her."

Jed stilled. "Was it Marshal Rodgers?" he asked.

Cal said, "I don't really know. I was not in the right state of mind to recollect details."

Jed said, "But you shot him in revenge anyway."

"No," Cal said, "it was Pete that did it, if anyone did. Went all crazy after Jenny got shot and started shooting back. Normally I would have stopped him, but…"

But why? He didn't know. "I was with Jenny until the end and then some. I didn't see anyone get shot, but I imagine a goodly number might've been. Like I said, I wasn't paying attention."

"Well," Jed said, "that might be true, might not. We're going to let the judge sort it out. Someone's got to pay for the marshal's death."

Cal snorted. "I reckon I paid enough that day. Besides, it wasn't me that did it. It was Pete."

Cal said, "Well, Pete's buried under a mountain. Not likely to be standing trial."

"So I get to swing in his place?" Cal said. "It ain't right for you to lock me up like this. Especially next to that thing." Cal nodded to the vampire in the box. "It oughta be drug out into the sunlight and killed."

"Reverend Graham is holding out that with Braga out of action, the prisoner might be saved."

"Nothing but second chances around here, Sheriff. Except for me, eh?"

Jed took off his hat and placed it on his lap. "I can't take a vampire to a judge, let alone hang him. The way I see it, that thing in the box is out of my jurisdiction and squarely in Reverend Graham's. You're still a man walking the patch of Earth I oversee, subject to the laws we're all bound by."

Cal snorted. "Saved your life, Jed. A bottle of whiskey and we're quits? Not by a long shot, Jed, not by a long shot."

Jed said, "This isn't between you and me. This is between you and the law. We're square, but you got to answer for your life's actions."

"I guess you'll just have to wait for yours, eh Jed?" He laid back down on the bunk. "May as well go on about your day, Sheriff. I got nothing left to say to you."

The chair scraped across the floor as Jed set it back against the wall. He paused half-way back to the office and said, "For what it's worth, Cal, I'm sorry."

And the hell of it was, Cal believed him.

Chapter Twenty-Eight

A COYOTE WAITED AT THE UNUSUAL HOLE IN THE GROUND, motionless in the moonlight but for its twitching ears, alert for larger predators. The hole was its favorite hunting spot, smelling of moisture, and though he couldn't fit down the hole and seek the water itself, the fat mice and occasional rat that dared venture out at night would sate the coyote's hunger and thirst in a few quick bites. There was one scratching its way up now, and it would be his.

His hackles raised as instincts sensed a larger predator. He cocked its ears from side to side and sniffed the air, straining for a sound or scent that would tell him from which direction the danger lie. Apart from the moist air and the scratching coming up the hole, the coyote detected nothing. He could only freeze, caught between urges to hide or run.

A snake that was not a snake emerged from the hole, smelling of nothing but earth and decay. A red-eyed stare fixed him in place. A blink later, the coyote died.

The questing tendril of flesh drained the coyote of its blood before heaving more of itself from the hole. Raw flesh oozed from the ground and coiled for several minutes before its tail emerged, trailing a rope. The flesh shuddered and began folding over on itself. White pebbles pulled together and crackled, forming long bones, a ribcage, and pelvis. Then the flesh flowed around it, rearranging itself into the shape of a man. The man sat up and drew breath, followed by a racked coughing.

Braga inhaled the night air, catching the lingering spoor of the men who tried burying him yesterday. He then turned his attention to the rope and pulled with the strength of a locomotive. A head appeared from the mine's ventilation shaft, balanced on top of a mass of twisted flesh whose tail in turn was tied around another's neck.

Braga heaved and drew his minions tied like sausage links one after the other until the last emerged, whereupon he untied the knotted ropes of hemp, sinew, and intestine. In the following minutes, the blobs untwisted and pushed out into human shapes, scattering what nocturnal wildlife remained into hiding. Madness and pain filled the blobs' eyes as each flowed across the ground and began coiling.

Despite the breaking and rebuilding of his form, Braga's wounds were mostly healed. For him, the long slumber had proven the more troublesome. After centuries of undead sleep, it was remarkable that he was able to recover his former strength within a few days. For the others reforming around him, the lack of experience marshaling their bodies' powers would be their limitation. They would need feeding to regain strength and full thinking minds. He scented the air and found the one he had marked, the one who had resisted his call. He sensed heartbeats around him; he sensed a meal.

Yesterday's attack had decimated Braga's flock, and only the strongest survivors had the courage and will to push through the agony, breaking themselves into flesh sacks small enough to win freedom via the mine's ventilation pipe. Those that did not, Braga left below to become mindless beasts who would tear each other apart until the last of them ossified in the dark from lack of nourishment, never to walk the surface again barring a miracle. And because the human's god had turned his back on those like Braga, there would be no miracles.

Among his minions, gasping and groaning on the ground, one began shrieking shortly after his lungs found the space to expand. Braga thumped the offender's head.

"Silence," he commanded. He reached within his minion's mind, this Alton Blackfeather, and made a few changes. While he couldn't take away the pain, he could control the minion's speech, so he removed its ability altogether. The others took note and stifled their own cries until the night returned to blessed quiet. Braga was surprised only the one had been driven mad. The peasantry of this time was made of stronger stuff than those of his youth.

Braga cocked his head and focused on the heartbeats cowering nearby. It was a moment's work to tear into the rabbit warren and collect them. The creatures were poor fare for his kind, but his minion's reformed bodies hungered again after such strain, and they fell on the prey with savagery.

The sycophant, Peter, was the first to recover, wiping a bloody smear from his lips with the back of his hand. "My lord," he said, "hunger pains me something powerful." Braga peered into the man's dreams and tasted his anger. A slow-cooked hatred for the first human Braga had marked, this Calvin, Peter's former liege lord, or headman, or whatever these peasants called themselves.

Braga said, "And so we will feed."

"More rabbits?" Peter barely hid his revulsion, hungry as he was.

"We will soon feast on the best fare: the blood of our enemies. Their scent lingers on the wind."

Peter looked at the moon, well along its downward path. "Surely it's too far to Sunset."

"The wildlife will blunt hunger's edge for tonight. On the morrow, we will feast on true prey while also replenishing our numbers from the ranches and farms along the march to Sunset."

"Lord, your strength may be such, but I can barely put one boot in front of the other," Peter said. "The sun will be up within hours."

Braga pointed at the abandoned mine office and moldering piles outside. "Gather the burlap and cut the carpets. I will teach you to fashion a plague cloak. Our journey will not be pleasant, but it can be done if we are careful and keep ourselves covered."

"Okay," Peter said. At Braga's flat stare he hastily amended, "At once, Lord Braga."

Peter organized the others and they worked through the night crafting cloaks to Braga's specifications, with short breaks for hunting. At first light, they donned their heavy garments and began the journey to Sunset.

Despite the plague cloaks, the sunlight made Braga and the others weak, barely dragging one foot in front of the other, hissing and cringing from the pock marks and blisters raised where seams and imperfections within the cloak's weave allowed pinpricks of light through. Still, they followed in a ragged line behind Braga as he led them like a hunting hound. He could taste the one Peter called Trigger. He could taste the man's fear and desperation on the air, beckoning to Braga stronger than any guiding beacon ever could.

Chapter Twenty-Nine

THE TOWN WAS NEARLY BACK TO NORMAL, APART FROM some minor chaos at the livery keeping wagons out on the streets. Jed had to play peacemaker between Hornsby and Graham when the reverend balked at having Hornsby's "war wagon" filled with vampire-slaying supplies parked in front of the church. Jed smoothed the situation over by swapping it out with the town's fire engine behind the cooper's shop, and putting off a showdown over the numerous brush piles and junk heaps around Sunset that Jed had planned on confronting Mayor Hornsby about while the town was still amiable to cleaning itself up.

The delay in fixing that particular problem irked him more than he'd admit to anyone but Sarah. The longer the delay, the more likely people's gumption would wane until the clutter became a permanent feature of Sunset, like the rusting heap of scrap rail and rotting ties on the far side of the train station that Jed had unsuccessfully bid the town clean up. The others hadn't seen it his way, believing it the railroad's mess and therefore its problem, not the town's.

Though now that he thought about it, he might

wrangle the territorial boys to take care of it when they came to clear the pass, which wouldn't happen until they fixed the telegraph, which wouldn't happen until the telegraph operator, Rumstead, sobered up enough to splice in and re-hang the wire. Someone had to keep Sunset running, and if Mayor Hornsby was too cowardly to tell others what's what, Jed would.

He stepped into his house and hung his rig on the wall along with his hat. The air inside was crisp, free of the dust, woodsmoke, and horse shit permeating his office. Jed thumbed the dust from his badge hung up his vest before walking with a soft tread across the floorboards. It was already past full dark, and three heads were asleep in the kids' room, Atticus, Melody, and now Molly. He closed the door softly and took care with his footsteps as he headed down the hall.

Jed closed the door to the bedroom and sat on the bed, staring at his boots. Sarah, already in her nightgown, watched him from her mirror as she brushed out her hair.

"Is it done?" she asked.

"It's done," Jed said. "The streets are clear, windows un-boarded, Rumstead is fixing to put the telegraph to rights next thing tomorrow, and everything's buttoned down at the jailhouse."

"Was it right, arresting him?" she asked.

Jed unbuttoned his collar. "Right or wrong, it's what the law obliges. It's a damn shame it can't reward the good but only punish the wicked. And I swore an oath to see it enforced."

Sarah paused her brushing. "Yes, that's exactly how you should say it, if someone asks. It shows you don't let personal sentiment get in the way of law and order."

"Meaning what?" he asked.

"Meaning when statehood comes, you'll be well placed

in the territorial government. You're a man who's level-headed, a man of integrity and stability who gets things done, regardless of personal affections. A fine example of leadership a new state needs."

"What? Like a marshal?" Jed said.

"Perhaps," she said. "Though I don't think a congressman or even a senator is beyond you."

Jed paused in the middle of taking his boots off. "I don't know about that," he said.

"You know perfectly well that we can't stay in Sunset for the rest of our lives. It was all a grand lark when were young and it was just ourselves against the frontier. But you've made your mark, and it's time for us move on to bigger things. Besides, you promised."

When he didn't respond, she added, "You can do just as much good, if not more, with an influential job. And the children's prospects will be greater as well."

Jed said, "Your prospects, you mean."

Sarah put the brush down. "Yes, mine, too. Ours together."

"I've got ties here," Jed said. "You might say I'm rooted, even."

Sarah came over to sit next to him on the bed. Soft fingers gripped his palm. "You were, but John's dead, Jedidiah. I loved him as a brother, too, but I think he'd agree with me. He'd want us to move on and make a fresh start."

Jed shook his hand loose from hers. "Don't put words in his mouth," he said. "He put too much into that ranch to have us just abandon it. If you want a fresh start, let's start there. We can keep that ranch going for his sake. Hell, for Molly's sake, too."

Sarah said, "You think Molly wants to go back to the place where her parents were killed? She screamed in her sleep last night, Jed. She kept screaming, eyes wide open but not seeing, Melody and Atticus petrified like she was possessed by the devil himself. Scared me half to death, too. You want to raise her in a palace of nightmares?"

"She'll get over it," Jed said.

"Because you can't? Don't you dare use Molly as an excuse. The best thing, if you were thinking as clearly about your family as you were about the law, the best thing for us is to get away from Sunset. You owe the living more than the dead. You owe your children a father, and your wife a husband who doesn't disappear in the night with a gun in his hand." She wrapped her arms around herself.

"You're just scared," Jed said and reached to squeeze her shoulder.

She shook him off. "Damn right I am. You would be too if you used a full measure of sense."

Jed blew out a breath. "We can work everything out on the ranch," he said.

"You don't know the first thing about ranching."

Jed felt the heat in his face and quickly turned from her before putting his boots back on. "I'll make it work," Jed said, "for Molly." The bedsprings squeaked as he rose and made for the hallway.

"You ever think she might not want that?" Sarah asked, but Jed had already closed the door and his boot steps drowned out her voice as he headed off to the jailhouse.

Chapter Thirty

SARAH KICKED THE SHEETS TO THE END OF THE BED. HER nightgown clung to her slick skin and her pillow wouldn't cool no matter how often she flipped it. She punched it down and turned over, telling herself not to ruminate over the argument with Jed and failing. After a good half hour of flopping around without respite from racing thoughts, she gave up and got out of bed to give the damp sheets a chance to dry.

She paced the room. Where had Jed gotten it in his head that he wanted to be a farmer? They had always talked about getting out of Sunset, and even he had admitted the town was wearing on him. Then he had promised her not two days ago about contacting the governor. A farmer? No, he couldn't mean it.

There was normally an ebb and flow to their spats, but this one felt different. Something in Jedidiah had changed. The death of his brother at the hand of these unnatural creatures was at the heart of it, she was sure. He'd moved with her out here after the war as much to leave the killing behind as to make a fresh start. Why didn't the same apply now? If the man would just speak plainly to her about it, she could help, but Jed probably didn't even know himself, which was the frustrating part. None of the men in Sunset talked about anything of substance, and she could only stand so many drunken stories about cattle and horses at the saloon. Jed would become like them, and she'd have to listen to the same stories at home, too.

Sarah got tired of pacing in the bedroom and decided to pace in the kitchen instead where she could at least take a glass of water from the sweating pitcher. She poured herself a glass and drank, the water's coolness in her throat not really easing her discomfort, but the idea of it helped.

She put the glass down and saw a doll on the floor in the corner. Molly's doll. Sarah stifled an oath and picked it up. She did not look forward to teaching Molly the rules of the house, especially keeping the home tidy. It had taken her forever to get her own kids to mind and would now have to teach another.

She did not know if she could be a mother of three. She knew in her head three would not be that much more to manage than two, but her heart spoke the greater truth. She would, of course, handle it all somehow, raising a child that was half stranger to her. In time those feelings might fade, and she'd see Molly no different than her own children, but it would take time. She was certain Molly would never call her "mother," and Sarah would never live up to Caroline's ghost. She shook her head and forced herself to think better of her nice. She would make it work.

Sarah tucked the doll under her arm and went to the kids' bedroom. She opened the door and discovered only two heads and an open window. Molly was gone.

Sarah threw on one of Jed's long coats over her nightgown, lit a lantern, and went on into the night. It was cooler outside, but it was clammy with humidity that teased a rain that never came. Still, it chilled her, so she gave the coat a couple buttons. She called in the night for Molly, while on the lookout for the white flash of a nightgown or mop of dark curls hiding behind a tree. The girl could not have gotten far.

Sarah imagined Molly had heard her and Jed argue. Oh, Lord, why did she say those things about her parents? Where the child had gotten in her head that running away was a good idea, she didn't know, but then again, Molly had been through a lot. She had to be terrified.

It felt like Molly's eyes were on her now, somewhere in the dark, a pressure that made Sarah's skin go prickly.

"Come on out, Molly," she called. "I know what you heard scared you, but it's going to all work out for the best, I promise!"

She held the lantern to the ground, trying and failing to find small footprints in the back yard. Her ears strained for any shifting of cloth or kicked stone, but the night was as silent as it was dark, with even the crickets holding their peace. Could the girl have gone any farther, into the hills? Sarah didn't know. She called again for Molly, with plenty of reassurances and promises, not really believing her own words but knowing she could set things straight in the morning light. Lies were things people told each other to feel better. If we didn't lie to ourselves, what's the point of going on? People had to believe that life would get better, and if the lies helped the time go by until it actually happened, then there was no real harm done.

She checked all the kids' normal haunts, where they played hide and seek, where they loitered when there were unfinished chores, but found nothing. Sarah *knew* Molly was nearby. She felt the girl's eyes on her.

Her heart leapt. Unless it wasn't Molly.

She looked across the yard once again, noting how far

she was from the house and the shotgun inside. Even farther from her derringers, which would be less than useless outside in the dark. The monsters moved so quick...

No. She was being craven. Jed said he killed them all, else he wouldn't have left her alone. Except he had done so before, hadn't he? So self-sure that he could meet the monsters out in the hills and one wouldn't kill her in her own bar by circling around behind...

Sarah whirled around and held the lantern to the darkness. Nothing. She shook her head to clear it as she chastised herself. Who was the lost girl now?

Lost girl. Of course! Molly wouldn't know her children's usual hiding places, therefore Molly would have found somewhere unusual to hide.

Sarah ranged farther out, past the line of trees marking the edge of the homestead, towards the old brush piles she forbid the children to play near because rattlers loved nesting there. As she turned, she saw a flash of white and sent a silent thanks above that she wouldn't have to get Jed and start another argument. She came upon a bundle wrapped in blankets.

"It's all right, Molly," she said. The poor girl had likely gotten to this far and didn't know where else to go. Sarah reached down and said, "It's okay, honey. Come on home."

She flipped back the blanket, and a face like shimmering molasses with red eyes stared back. She had just enough time to scream before she felt a pinch at her neck and the world faded.

Chapter Thirty-One

SARAH WOKE UP BACK IN HER BED, HER NIGHTGOWN STILL stuck to her skin, but the moon had climbed higher in the sky. She had dreamt Molly had run away and gotten herself eaten by Jed's monsters. This damned heat. Sarah toyed with the idea of going back to sleep, but the dream had been so vivid, she had to exorcise it completely or sleep might never come. Sarah decided the first step was getting up and checking on Molly just to be sure, but her body felt so weak.

"You are lucky that I have chosen you," said a deep voice. "It is better that I have chosen you rather than feed you to my minions."

Sarah's heart lurched at the oily black figure standing at the end of her bed. Her hand automatically reached for the derringer on the bed stand and swung it towards him. The figure, dressed in a long leather duster and wide-brimmed hat, inclined his head, but did not move otherwise.

"I am Lord Braga, and your tiny weapon cannot harm me, Sarah Scott," he said. His misshapen face, with off-centered red eyes floating over a bulbous nose, split into a needle-toothed grin.

Sarah remembered how ineffective the derringer had been against the other vampire at the bar. And, despite the gun's feather weight, her arm began shaking. She lowered the weapon and clutched it to her chest.

"Where are my children?" she asked.

"I sent the others to fetch them," Braga said. Sarah pushed herself higher up in bed, feeling a fever's heat and chill's tickle simultaneously racing through her chest and limbs. Braga seemed to read her thoughts.

"You are transforming into a higher being," he said. His gaze drifted in a way that made her reach to her neck where fingertips found two puckered wounds. Braga unhinged his jaw wide and snaked a tongue across his fangs. She couldn't fight the compulsion of reaching out with her tongue and discovering the uncomfortable heft and sharpness of elongated canines within her own mouth.

"A monster like you," she countered. "Ugly and misshapen."

It was literally an eye blink. Braga lurched as if he was going to attack her, a snarl with fangs and claws, within inches of her throat, but in the next eye blink, it was as if nothing had happened. He was back at the end of her bed, calm, once again studying her.

"Maybe we should have your children visit after all," Braga said. He gestured and another one of the vampires brought them in. Both children stood glassy-eyed in their sleeping gowns, uncomprehending, indifferent to the terrible monsters around them. Sarah's heart lurched and she stumbled out of the bed for them, but her legs would not support her and she fell to the floor. Braga was there in an instant, catching her and setting her back into bed.

"Fear not, they are under my command. Their minds

are asleep. They are only here to assure your cooperation. If you like, they can be your reward to do with as you please once your transformation is complete," he said.

The warmth was fading, and a growing numbing cold at her fingertips and toes began spreading up her arms and legs.

"Think of this not as an end, but as a beginning, a way to keep your family together and grow your prestige, even keeping your youth so that all your gains will not fade," he said.

Something in the way he was talking, she knew he was lying, or at least hiding the full truth. He was desperate for something from her, but she could not fathom it. Something dear to her, she sensed.

"And what about my soul?" she said. "The Reverend Graham and Jedidiah seemed to think that your souls are damned."

Braga shrugged. "Heaven and hell are not concerns for those of us who will never die," he said.

Sarah felt the change coming like a wave of ice water about to break over her head. The derringer was still in her hand, resting against her chest. It would be only a moment to turn it upon her own heart and fire. She could die as she was now, she knew, still human.

She looked to the kids and quailed. She couldn't leave them in Braga's clutches, but would they still love her as a vampire? Would she still love them? Already her mind was splitting. Her mind was still partially her own, a wife and a mother, a human, a creature of light. The other part of her mind was becoming a predator that looked upon her children and saw only prey. After the change, would she still protect them, or would she feed upon them? Would they die at her own hand? Would it be worse for them to be torn apart by monsters, or by their own mother?

She gripped the derringer tighter to her chest as the frigid wave swept across her spine. The room darkened and she was trapped within herself surrounded by alien, whispering thoughts. Was the whisper Braga or herself? They whispered if she left now, she would be abandoning her responsibility. She didn't come this far just to give up now. She reinvented herself before coming out west, and she could do so again. Yes.

She let the derringer drop from her numb fingers and let the wave break upon her. As the shock swept through her flesh, a tiny part of her mind cried out, convinced she had made the wrong choice, but it quickly faded along with the last of her body's heat.

SARAH AWOKE and looked upon the room with new eyes. Details jumped out at her. The moonlight glowed silver, showing her everything within the room yet the shadows remaining sharp, like paper cutouts. A fly droned around the room in lazy curves, slow as if it were caught in honey. Braga's knobby fingers snatched it from the air as easily as reaching for a grape but with a speed she had not been able to follow until now.

Her lord smiled and cocked an ear. Sarah closed her eyes. Her nose detected the musty damp, acrid leather, and iron-tinged dirt clinging to Lord Braga's coat. Her ears picked out trees creaking outside the house and leaves scraping across each other. Within her was a quiet center, like a calm pool of water that couldn't be disturbed, not even by the heartbeat she no longer had. Instead, she heard the tiny hearts beating within the children, growing louder every moment.

A cold gnawing at her stomach grew also, and she opened her eyes.

"You are fortunate I chose to ease your transformation and postpone your feeding madness, yet feed you must," Braga said, and pushed the children forward.

Sarah considered them, remembering her old self that used to love these children and would have done anything to protect them, but that's all it was, a memory. She felt more strongly about feeding from them, but stopped herself, putting the predator at bay for a moment.

"We will need the children to convince Jedediah to join us," she said. Her plans required a family, and when she had her family secured to her lord's service, they would be unstoppable.

Braga smiled as if he caught her thoughts. "You have strength, Sarah Scott. You will become the face of a new empire, its beloved queen, while I guide you and your husband from the shadows." His needle-toothed grin filled her with awe.

Sarah gasped as Braga overwhelmed her senses and painted a picture directly in her mind's eye. A fine manor house with servants waiting upon heads of industry and government congregating and seeking out her guidance and support as she cultivated power.

The vision broke as a hunger pang struck her.

"Where is the third child, Molly?" she asked.

"That one I promised to Peter," Braga said.

"Pity." Sarah could have fed on that one.

Chapter Thirty-Two

CAL SAT IN HIS CELL, SPLAYING HIS HAND IN THE moonlight and making animal shadows against the wall, thinking about how they were going to hang him. He contemplated his last meal. Should he go with something that was his favorite, like chicken fried steak or grilled trout that someone might ruin for him? Or should he go for something exotic? Quail under glass had to be good, right? Nah, they'd probably give him chicken and he wouldn't know any better. It was hard thinking about food, though. The vampire in the box next door was giving off foul whiffs like a tannery works. He should think about what his last words would be. Maybe…

The door to the jail swung open and Deputy Otto cried out before thumping to the floor. Cal watched Pete's lean shadow drift down the hall with Molly in tow.

"Surprised to see me?" Pete asked. "You can't keep me down forever, Trigger." He saw Cal's eyes on Molly. "Look what I found hiding outside. Thought of quenching my thirst then and there, but you know I hate eating in the dark all by my lonesome." The girl was rigid with fear but still wriggled and struggled to get loose from Pete's grip. Pete didn't pay her attention as he took a look around the cells. "I have to admit, I'm surprised you're locked up here and not riding around with your new friends, Trigger. You have a falling out?"

"Figures you'd manage to worm your way out somehow," said Cal. "As for my current lodgings, I'm in here for what you did in that town outside Yuma."

"Woodland? That was all you, Cal," Pete said with a smile. "You set it up, then you and your weak stomach went to pieces."

"Jenny was dying, Pete."

Pete's smile faded. "Yes, and it was your fault," he said. The box in the next cell started rattling. "You put Jenny in harm's way and were somehow surprised when she got shot before proceeding to go to pieces when she needed you the most. I watched the whole thing happen from the outside and couldn't do nothing because protecting her was *your job*, Cal. She picked the wrong man. I would have kept her safe. I wouldn't have been distracted inside that bank, and I wouldn't have gone all soft in the aftermath with your dumbass 'no killing' rules."

Cal swallowed his bubbling anger. Pete was trying to get him all worked up, but he wouldn't give him the satisfaction. "That rule kept the law off us," Cal said.

Pete looked around the jail house. "Worked out real well for you, too. Was it worth it, Trigger? In the end, the only one who got revenge for Jenny, killing all the men who did it?" He tapped his chest. "Me. I killed all of 'em, Cal, except the one truly responsible."

Cal knew Pete was just poking at what Cal had told himself over the years before burying it deep. His fingertips brushed the calico lump in his pocket and his eyes fell on Molly, about to become another one if his failures. Except

Cal knew he was a dead man already, which might be enough to save the kid before he bought it. He might give Molly her chance at escape if he riled Pete, who fancied himself a smart man.

"You aren't making a lick of sense, Pete. Listen to yourself," he said.

"I'm not?" Pete said. His lip curled and a pale tongue polished a fang. Pete's gaze drifted over to the other cell and with a grin, he pushed Molly inside it, locking it behind her.

Cal stood. He'd miscalculated again. "Let the girl go, Pete, she's been through enough. It's me you're sore with."

"Oh, you're a bit right about that," Pete said, "But not altogether right. She's just here to focus your attention." The box next door began scraping across the floor as the beast within it went wild and threw itself against its sides. "I bet he's hungry, eh, Trigger? I wonder if he has enough mind left to understand me. And if I weaken just one link in these chains like so…" Pete stretched the chain link with his bare hands, which popped with a squeal. "It might be that he might work his way free."

The chest began to clap and rumble. Molly screamed.

Cal reached through his bars for Pete but only caught air. "You were a mean bastard before, Pete, but never like this. How's it feel being a monster?"

"You're trying to rattle me, Trigger. It won't work." He leaned closer, just outside Cal's reach. "How's this feel? You put Jenny into a situation just like this. You can see it all about to unfold but can't do a thing about it, can you?"

The box lid hinged open, and the vampire broke free, red eyes wild. A miasma of corrupted flesh made Cal's last meal rise in his throat. The thing spun in the moonlight, withered flesh sagging like curtains and patches of hair falling out of his scalp. The vampire's skin was translucent, light enough to almost see the bones beneath it. Its talons were broken from scratching the iron casket's innards. It took one look at Molly and lunged for her. She shrieked as she ran under its clumsy arms to Cal's side of the cell, shaking the bars between them. The vampire lunged at her, tripping over its own feet. Cal reached through the bars and caught it by the throat. Taloned hands swiped and clutched for the girl, but Cal's grip held. Even as weak as it was, Cal knew the strain would sap his strength in seconds.

Pete cackled and taunted, "Not easy, is it, Trigger? It's going to get loose, we don't tire like you." True to Pete's words, Cal's grip was already burning, so he did the only thing he could think of. He jerked back and grappled with a forearm against the vampire's mouth as it struggled against him. Smashed its head back against the bars. It snarled and its jaws clamped down. An icy spike followed by a pleasant numbness spread through his arm. The vampire fed and Cal's world started going gray at the edges. Then Pete ripped the hinges off the door to Cal's cell and grabbed him from behind.

"Think you're getting off that easy, Trigger?" Pete said. Then, to the other vampire, he said, "Go on, *amigo*."

Pete wrenched the vampire from Cal's arm. The wild vampire had enough of Cal's blood in it so now it appeared skinny rather than starving. It rounded on Molly and surged forward.

A gun barked twice behind him. Bullets hit flesh leaving the telltale smoking holes of holy ammo.

Cal could feel Pete's head swinging around, and he took his opportunity to give a mighty shove and break Pete's hold, but Pete was too strong. Cal hooked a leg behind and bucked to the side. Pete's weight shifted to one foot. Cal kicked out, sending them both tumbling to the floor. Pete landed on top of him, hands going to Cal's throat and squeezing. Then Pete went still as something shuddered through him and pressed against Cal's breastbone. Pete's eyes rolled up and a moment later, his weight slid aside with a bloody stake poking through his chest. Cal found Jed kneeling beside Pete, giving the stake a final twist. Cal patted his own chest, finding missing buttons and bare skin scratched, not pierced.

"I appreciate the help, Jed, but you could have killed me, too," Cal said.

"Nah, I used one of them shitty cedar stakes. Wouldn't have done more than scratch you." Jed looked to Molly, who was edging around the still vampire, heading for the door.

She looked at Jed and said, "I tried to get them to come with me, but they didn't believe me. Monsters are all headed for the house."

Jed's face paled, and his hands had the slightest tremor. He tossed a ring of keys to Cal and said, "Get her to Graham over at the church."

"I'll come help you," he said, but Jed shook his head.

"You're in no shape to fight." He headed into the office and began reloading his pistols.

"I'll be wanting my guns regardless," Cal said.

Jed nodded to Cal's rig hanging on the wall as he tucked two stakes at the small of his back. "Get Graham to bless your bullets. I'll meet you back at the church."

Chapter Thirty-Three

THE CHURCH STOOD AT THE END OF THE STREET, A WARM glow spilling through the double doors and windows while the tinkling of a piano accompanied the few parishioners God-fearing enough to attend Graham's impromptu service. Or so Cal gathered from Deputy Otto's jawing as he led them from the jailhouse. Molly clutched Cal's hand near to breaking, and her dark head kept swiveling around to glance behind them every dozen steps.

"You'll be safe inside," Cal said as he double-checked the shadows between buildings himself.

"You don't know that," Molly said.

Cal couldn't find it within him to bullshit the kid, so he went for a near-truth. "I know the reverend is mighty rough on vampires and too ornery to kill. If I were looking for a place to hole up, that's where I'd go."

"I want to leave," she whispered.

"I hear you," Cal said.

Some sun-stroked fool had parked a wagon carrying the town's fire engine before the church steps: a man-high brass urn surrounded by piping, sporting a tightly coiled hose with fittings that shone like new and smelled of fresh grease, making Cal wonder if perhaps the service was intended as some sort of dedication ceremony for the contraption. It seemed to Cal that Graham's time would be better spent on man than machine, especially now.

The music stopped as they mounted the steps, and Reverend Graham's voice boomed through the open doors. The preacher stood front and center with his empty sleeve cuffed and pinned and standing behind a lectern facing the handful of townsfolk dotting only a couple of the church's two dozen pews.

Graham still looked a fright, face sallow and dark circles around his eyes, leaning slightly to the left, still not used to compensating for his missing arm's weight. "Brothers and sisters, I stand before you today grateful more than ever for your fellowship during these past tribulations…"

Graham's weary grin faded as Cal entered. Heads turned, and an old woman recoiled. Jed realized he and Molly still had blood splattered on their clothes. "You'll be wanting to hold off on the celebration, Reverend. They're back."

"The Indians?" someone said.

"I thought it were Crows," said another.

Cal shook his head and wondered how much to tell them.

"Not Indians, monsters!" Molly said, tiny voice loud in the open-beamed interior. "Dead men with fangs and claws!"

Someone broke out laughing, trailing off when he realized neither Jed, Otto, nor Graham corrected the child.

Otto twisted his hat in his hands. "There never were any Indians. The sheriff could hardly believe it himself, me neither, when the one that busted up the telegraph office took a load of buckshot to the chest and bullet to the eye and was still movin'? I started believin' real quick. Saw the feller's holes seal up and life come back to him as we chained him up."

"Bullshit," the laughing man said, then murmured, "Apologies, Reverend."

Graham hung his head. "Horace, it was a coven of those foul creatures that took not only my arm, but the lives of those brave souls of the posse and that little girl's family. I had thought we entombed them for eternity in the Dexter Mine, but we failed."

"And there's likely a mess of them coming this way," Cal said.

The room stilled until Horace asked, "Where is the sheriff?"

"He's coming," Otto said.

The townsfolk looked at each other, murmuring with no few looking as if they might bolt. Cal stepped onto a pew and harshened his voice. "We need to slow them down until we can shore up the town and the sheriff comes back," he said. "These monsters, these vampires, feast on blood. Ours, if they can get it, but I reckon most will take what's closest at hand. At least at first." He looked over the shocked faces. "We got anything close to town that'll distract 'em? Cattle? Sheep?"

"What about goats?" someone said. "Cleburne's got a handful just outside town."

Cal nodded. "That'll do. Stake 'em out, all around, so we'll know which way they're coming from."

"And what do we tell Cleburne?"

"Sheriff will pay him for any that gets killed," Cal said.

"He will?" murmured Otto.

"He'd better," Cal said. "Now here's what we're going to do."

Chapter Thirty-Four

JED JUMPED OFF HIS HORSE AND CHARGED THROUGH HIS home's open door, guns drawn. He expected to find blood and destruction, but everything was in its place. He found the scene uncanny, like he and the house were strangers to one another. The door to the kids' room yawned open, the room empty. He kept his guns fixed on the closed bedroom door down the hall and advanced, spurs jangling with each step across the floorboards.

Sarah was at the mirror, painting her lips and wearing her best dress, a narrow-waisted cut in satin that rippled between sapphire and near-black in the light. The kids were tucked in bed, asleep. A musky smell in the air tickled at his brain but quickly faded.

"Welcome home, Jedediah," Sarah said.

"I found Molly in town, plus a—" Jed said, and holstered his guns. Then he stopped to consider the kids. "—one of those outlaws that I was after. She said there might be others coming this way."

"Everything's fine here, Jed," she said. The lilt in her voice was one he normally welcomed but hadn't expected its use after coming barreling in with guns drawn. "She snuck out, and after a thorough search, I surmised she must have gone off to find her hero uncle in town. Where else would she go?"

"She said the vampires had come back."

Her voice cooled. "She would."

Jed glanced to the room's corners, then lowered himself to look under the bed. "And the kids?" he asked.

"They were scared when they woke up to find Molly gone," she said. "They thought she was stolen by those Apaches you had the town all worked up about, so I let them sleep in here. And then I couldn't go back to sleep after traipsing around outside looking for her, so I decided to play a bit." She turned and smoothed her dress before regarding him. "Do you like it?"

"They're awfully still," Jed said with a nod to the children. "We should get them somewhere safer in town."

"They're very tired," she said, brushing a stray blonde lock behind her ear.

"Are you okay, Sarah?" he said.

"Why wouldn't I be, Jed?" she said, and turned her attention to two hat boxes at her feet.

Something had clearly spooked his wife into an odd hysteria, something that needed a doctor, not a lawman. He decided he would have to treat her like a spooked horse, one that might jump in any direction without warning. Jed crossed the room and put his hand on her shoulder, as he forced a smile to his face. "You look like a dream, Mrs. Scott. Would you fancy a moonlight ride in the surrey?" She gave him a haughty smile and put a hand over his.

Jed sucked in a breath. "You're freezing."

"Am I? I feel perfectly comfortable," she said. He squeezed her shoulder and looked at her though the mirror. Except it showed only his arm hanging in midair, with the kids sleeping behind him. He went for his gun, but Sarah's grip squeezed with a strength that ground his knuckle bones together and sent him to his knees. She rose from the chair, snatching the guns from his holsters, and leveling them at his head.

"You're too late, Jed," she said. "Lord Braga has already made his introductions."

Jed's gaze went to the kids. "The children," he said.

"Asleep until I awaken them. Otherwise unharmed."

"I can get you help, Sarah," he said. "Reverend Graham thinks—"

"Come now, Jed," Sarah said. Red specks flared within her eyes, and he discovered he couldn't tear himself from her stare. "My soul's been stained, never to come clean again. Remember?"

"I was wrong," Jed said.

"The great Jedediah Scott? Hardly." Then the red glow left her eyes as she lowered the guns a little, leaving only her icy blues. She pulled her gown to expose two bruised punctures at her neck. "It was this or lose the family. You understand? Everything we built would die. Why am I always the one that makes sacrifices, Jed?"

"Because we don't always get what we want, Sarah. A man can only try the best he can." He knew he'd screwed up when the red came back to her eyes.

"On that we agree," she said. She cocked the hammers on both guns.

"You gonna shoot me?" Jed asked.

She shook her head. "How could I shoot my husband?"

"I don't rightly know if you're still the wife I married."

"For better or worse, richer or poorer," Sarah said. "You've been a man of your word up until now, Jedediah.

If you love me, you'll do right by me and not resist what has to happen."

The words stabbed through him. She had him to rights. He had always made hard choices, and for the love of this woman, he wouldn't slack now, even if it cursed his soul. Jed sighed, then nodded. "I do and I will. But if I do this, we leave. And keep the children out of this."

A smile pulled at the corners of her mouth. "If you feel the same way after the change, by all means," she said, and beckoned him to stand.

Jed took to his feet, opened his arms, and said, "Get on with it." As she came to embrace him, perfume filled his head, reminding him of their first courting. "I loved you," he said.

"I loved you, too," she replied before biting down.

Sweet numbness flowed through him, then a euphoria he hadn't felt since their first night together, one he'd never forgotten. He never wanted it to end, but instead he reached behind his back and grasped the stake's rough edges. It pulled hardly at all as it drove through her. Sarah arched back with a gasp, surprise and betrayal on her face. The red in her eyes didn't fade.

"Till death do us part," Jed said and lowered her to the floor.

He managed to get the kids out of the house without them seeing the state of their mother. He worried they'd been bespelled or drugged somehow or that Sarah had lied about biting them, but he couldn't find any marks on them, and their senses came back to them along the way into town. Questions were asked, but they knew not to press his silence. His mind was numb, and he refused to dwell on what he'd just done. He owed his wife — late wife — that much. She'd have wanted him to get the children safe and carve out her revenge on the hides of those responsible.

He would avenge her.

He repeated that to himself to blot out the memory of her limp body on the bedroom floor and the red-stained water his hands left in the wash basin.

Jed arrived at the church, met by Cal, who had a new bandage around his forearm and a drunken stagger to his gait. Molly's black curls peeked out behind him.

"Just you three, then?" Cal asked.

The tightness in his chest that he'd held down traveled to his throat and the blubbering weakness behind it threatened to leak out. He nodded instead.

"Take them inside to see the Reverend, would you, Molly?" Cal said.

Jed eased his children down from the saddle and Molly darted out and led them by the hand to where Reverend Graham was awkwardly nailing boards across the church windows one-handed.

Cal tapped at his neck. "That going to be okay?"

Jed pulled his kerchief higher to cover the puncture wounds. "Ain't bothering me."

"It'll fester, believe me," Cal said.

"It's a problem for tomorrow."

Cal sniffed and shook his head. "I guess it is. Let's get to it."

Chapter Thirty-Five

As they left the church, Jed was more taciturn than usual, one-word answers to Cal's questions little more than grunts. From what Cal could string together, Braga had hit Jed's home, and Sarah hadn't made it.

"Sorry," Cal said, but Jed didn't seem to hear him. Cal noted the blood trickling from underneath the handkerchief at Jed's neck when a series of screams echoed through the hills outside town.

"Those didn't sound human," Jed said.

"We sent a rider to some fella name of Cleburne to let his goats out to distract 'em."

"I hope for your sake Cleburne got free of 'em," Jed said. "You go to the cooper shop, break out the barrel staves. I'll grab guns from the office and meet you."

"You sure you won't—?" But Jed was already off. Cal debated running after him and helping himself to a few fancy guns from Jed's office, but decided he would follow orders.

Cal rummaged through the cooper shop and found a pile of loose barrel staves that someone in town had cut down for stakes. Cal didn't know what kind of wood it was, he just knew that it felt solid in his hands, sturdier than cedar and a hell of an improvement. He heard a footstep behind him, and he whirled, gun leading, to find Jed entering without a care that he almost got his fool head blown off. The cavalry saber swung from his waist, reflecting light with each of Jed's heavy steps as he carried a wooden box across the room and set in a corner before covering it with a tarp.

"What's in the box?" Cal asked.

"Insurance. Not much, but there's more to do before they arrive. With me, Cal."

They left through the back of shop to what Jed called "the mayor's damn wagon" filled with anti-vampire supplies and set aside after the previous day's cleanup. Jed and Cal pushed it into the street.

"I reckon this wagon has everything we'll need to wage war," Cal said.

Jed looked at him funny and said, "I don't expect this to be anything so civilized."

They collected their horses from the church, where Jed addressed the assembled crowd. "Those that can handle a gun, do so. Keep them vampires' heads down! You other men, stand by with the stakes and stab 'em in the heart. The rest of you, hole up in the church and pray for daylight."

"How can we hope to stand up to demons, sheriff?" someone called out.

Jed nodded at Cal. "Because we got one of our own! This here's Trigger Jones, which means we've got heaven and hell covered between us. And there ain't no standing up to that."

Scared faces turned his way, and Cal gave them his best outlaw stare.

"Trigger and I will take the lion's share, y'all just keep 'em off our backs."

A man shouted and pointed down the street. Cal turned in time to see shadows flitting in from the opposite side of town into the saloon. Wood splintered and a startled cry died on the wind.

Jed guided his horse to the middle of the street and gestured for Cal to ride behind and to the side. Cal resisted the urge to wipe at the cold sweat tickling between his shoulder blades and kept his eyes wandering, watching out for figures slinking in the shadows and hoping that he wouldn't take a stray bullet from some trigger-happy farmer or shopkeeper when it came to it.

Jed stopped his horse short of the saloon and called out, "Braga, time you and I settled up." No sound came from the saloon, and with each passing second, Jed sat taller and straighter in the saddle. When it became clear there would be no response, Jed called out again with a parade-ground crispness. "You're quite fine, I must say, at hiding behind others, Braga. Perhaps in your time such was called leadership. However, in the New World, you'll find men respond best to those who lead by example."

And get their damned heads blown off, Cal mentally added.

Jed shifted and his mouth quirked as if he heard Cal's thoughts. "That is, unless you're a damned coward."

"Damned, perhaps," said a deep voice. A shadow moved within the saloon, approaching the batwing doors with the scraping tread of hardened nails on wood. Braga pushed through the doors and stepped onto the boardwalk, long arms poking through a tattered duster and red eyes glowing under his hat's straight brim. "Am I not afforded a trial, sheriff?" His lips peeled back from his snake-fanged maw that sent Cal's heart hammering.

Jed's hands dropped the reins, drifting over his guns and holding steady. "We're past that, Braga."

Braga let out a gurgling cackle. "Revenge? I can taste your thoughts, Sheriff. The sweet tang of revenge hiding behind the righteousness of a godly fool. The nature of man has not changed during my slumber." His eyes tracked the townsfolk poking heads out from behind the wagon and peering between the boarded windows of the church, and he cackled again. "Though in my time, men built their cities around cathedrals, for it was the center of their lives. Here it is not the case. Your flock will discover their church is a poor sanctuary, for they will find no protection there. The people of Sunset worship no god but progress, whose temple resides in the pride of place. By rights, your people should have barricaded themselves in the..." Braga's gaze drifted over Cal's shoulder to the center of town. "...train station." Braga stumbled over the word "train," as if he had only just learned it.

Jed dismounted and stood in the middle of the street. Braga's face split wider into a lopsided smile and he stepped off the boardwalk. The ancient vampire moved with an insouciant grace, slow but in perfect balance, coming to a stop opposite Jed, maybe twenty paces distant, Cal reckoned.

He and Jed stared each other down, Jed pulling back his duster and holding a hand over his Peacemaker in that odd cavalry cross draw that seemed to work for him, but Cal couldn't see how it could be any kind of fast. Braga stood tall with his long fingers flexing, arms spread wide. They stared at each other when a shadow tugged at the corners of Cal's vision. A raggedy form gathered itself on general store's roof and prepared to leap on Jed from behind.

It wasn't even a moment's thought when Cal drew and

fired. Jed and Braga both exploded into action. Jed drew faster than Cal could follow, an eye blink, if that. Braga threw himself to the side, but Cal couldn't see if Jed had shot true or merely winged Braga because Jed swiveled and fired over Cal's head, sending a creeping vampire crashing to the ground.

Lord Braga fled back into the saloon, clutching his ribs as his horde erupted from the shadows.

Chapter Thirty-Six

Jed and Cal split up, each taking a building as vampires fled the saloon. Cal's body went cold and feverish simultaneously, sending shivers through his limbs even as sweat poured down his face. He would have to make it work somehow.

He staggered through the doorway, both guns drawn, stakes pressing into his back. His Navy .36s swept on their own accord to the staircase just as the vampire crashed over a railing. His first shot took it to the shoulder, the next one to the throat as it fell through the air. Cal rolled to the side, and the floorboards cracked and splintered as the vampire landed where he once stood, claws going to his throat. In one motion, Cal rolled forward, grabbing a stake from the small of his back and driving it through the vampire's chest, ending it.

Cal swept through the back rooms just to make sure, but he sensed that no one else was coming. Soon he was out the door and down the boardwalk into the next building, where a vampire was feeding on a middle-aged woman, her blonde hair tight in a bun. Her hands were wrapped around a pair of bloodied scissors. The vampire was so engaged it didn't even turn when Cal stabbed it from behind. He pulled the monster off its victim, but the woman was already dead.

"Sorry," he murmured, but she couldn't hear him. He drove his other stake through her, just in case.

The chill wore off, as did the tremors in his fingers. Cal waited for the nausea to hit him, feeling poorer than ever, numb like he'd been wrapped in cotton. But his stomach didn't spasm and guns were still barking outside, so he grit his teeth and moved on.

Jed was across the street, firing at vampires on rooftops and directing the townsfolk, trying to concentrate their fire and flush the vampires out. The last of the women and children ducked into the church and the main doors slammed shut with a thud.

"You alright?" Jed asked. "You look like shit."

"I'll be fine," he growled.

"Then get on your horse, Cal," Jed said.

Cal found Rocky and after several attempts, mounted up. Jed was already beside him on Cactus, leading him behind the livery. Sharpened poles, about ten feet long, leaned against the wall. Jed snatched one up in a gallop and Cal immediately understood. He swung low and grabbed one too, tucking it under his arm.

They circled around the street at a gallop where the wounded vampires were charging Mayor Hornsby and the townsfolk at the war wagon. Cal spurred Rocky on as Jed swept right, Cal left. He lowered his lance. Cal hadn't executed a cavalry charge in the war. They had trained for it, but this was the first time he had ever done it in battle. The lance took the vampire in the chest, impact tearing the weapon from his hands as it skewered the monster through the rib cage. Cal made to dismount and finish it with stakes, but Hornsby had already rushed out and plunged a pair of barrel staves into its chest. The rest of the vampires scattered and Jed drew his saber, running one down and lopping off its head. Cal circled Rocky back to the livery and took up another lance as more gunfire popped around him.

Screams rose from the church where a vampire had circled around and now clawed at the boarded window. Nails squealed as a board came loose and Cal touched heels to Rocky's flanks, knowing that he was going to enter a charnel house if the vampires got inside. Then it screeched, hit by a powerful water stream. The vamp's pause and the confusion gave Cal the extra seconds to close, and Rocky's bulk knocked it from the window. From inside, he spied the town's fire engine, taking on more water, and Graham holding out his good arm blessing the water tank. Then his view was blocked off as those inside brought up another board, followed by the sound of hammers pounding nails.

Cal's nostrils filled with decay as the vampire dissolved in the holy water puddle around Rocky's hooves. He turned to join Jed near the war wagon.

Chapter Thirty-Seven

JED WATCHED CAL COMING FROM THE MELTED VAMPIRE AND mentally nodded to himself. He had the measure of the filthy beasts now. Braga was trying to distract him while outflanking, but the monster was still stuck in the Middle Ages, and he'd just run into the equivalent of a Gatling gun in a fortified position with cavalry support. But it wouldn't be enough to save Sunset. The rest of the vampires had disappeared, but he could hear them scuttling in the dark, regrouping.

Cal came riding up on his Appaloosa, listing in the saddle and likely wounded. "Report," Jed said.

The other man bristled but said, "The Reverend's got it all handled at the church so long as the water holds out."

"It should, so long as he's judicial with the spraying," Jed said. "That machine's meant to be crewed by six men, not a one-armed priest and a gaggle of women and children."

"They'll make it work," Cal said.

Jed turned to the street without a word and wondered where the next attack might come from.

"What are you thinking, Sheriff?" Cal asked. The other four men at the war wagon turned to listen in.

"Eyes front. Keep looking for targets," Jed admonished them. Damn, sloppy discipline. What would win the battle? Then he realized he had just missed something Cal had said. It probably didn't matter. Jed kept watching the street, quiet now. Cal repeated himself but Jed told him to shut up. Where were they? You could almost hear Braga's whispers on the wind, directing the monsters somehow.

There came a squeal of metal on the hilltop. Of course. Jed cursed himself a fool.

"What the hell's that?" Cal said.

Mayor Hornsby's face paled. "The windmill," he said.

Cal started reloading his pistols and asked, "So?"

Hornsby pointed. "The railroads put it up there because it was almost always windy and the downhill run builds water pressure. It's what's supplying the…" The pipe squealed, and there was a giant crash, followed by water gurgling into the night.

"Move this wagon back," Jed said. "You'll have to defend the church closer. The town's a loss."

The mayor piped up as if to say something but then thought better of it and gestured to his men. "Move the wagon, boys. Then say your prayers and pass the ammunition."

Cal snapped his revolver cylinders closed and nodded to Jed before riding away towards the busted pipes, shouting he'd cut off any vampires crawling down the cliff face trying to flank them. Jed stayed with the wagon in case Braga tried circling around the other side. The men heaved and rolled the wagon nearly up to the church's doors, from which a crack opened, and Graham's voice asked Jed what happened.

"Looks like your water feed's done, Reverend. You'll

have to make do with whatever's in the tank. There's a mess of them still about, including Braga."

The man looked struck for a moment, then raised his chin. "The Lord will provide all that is needed," Graham said.

Jed wasn't so certain about that, but then again, he had to believe the preacher knew his business when it came to miracles.

More shots barked from the hillside. Jed rode out, sheathing his sword in favor of his repeater. Bullets whizzed past his head, but he found it within himself not to care. He felt like he was dead already. He wondered if Sarah was laughing at him or cursing him, then figured she was probably nowhere at all, having surrendered her soul to the monsters. Just gone. No punishment. No reward. Just nothing. He felt utterly alone. He looked around, mechanically shooting targets as they appeared.

Vampire to his left.

Sight, shoot, lever.

Vampire to his right.

Sight, shoot, lever.

A couple of them trying to lasso the defenders behind the war wagon and those that had poked out guns from church windows.

Sight, shoot, lever. Repeat.

He had the odd detached feeling like he had nothing left in common with any of them, vampire or human.

Click. Time to reload.

He fed the cartridges in by touch as he guided Cactus in using his knees.

Of course, he was probably going to hell too for killing his wife unless the good Lord saw it as he did. But who was he to say? He killed his wife.

Sight. Shoot. Lever.

The mother of his children.

Sight. Shoot. Lever.

Maybe she wasn't herself when Braga came, or maybe she hadn't been herself for a long time. Years, maybe. And he hadn't seen it until the very end. He hadn't. And he wasn't feeling anything, apart from a growing chill in his bones mixing with a fever tingling at his scalp.

A vampire appeared to his right, sprinting from the scrub. He set the repeater against the saddle horn and drew his saber, turning Cactus and sending him charging, easily catching up with the fast bastard. The sword rose and fell, another vampire took a swipe at the horse itself, but Jed's horse was war trained. Cactus avoided the creature with a dancing step to the side.

Jed's pressing knees and a straightening in the saddle telegraphed his intent, and the horse spun in a circle, adding its weight behind Jed's blow, separating the vampire's head from its shoulders and sending it sailing into the night.

It was the only thing he had really been good at, battle. It was the mistress he had thrown Sarah over for, and now that he had her all to himself, he found her embrace lacking, as he had before. The only thing that kept him from the bleakness of it all was Sarah. And now she was gone.

He saw Cal harassing a vampire crawling on a church roof. His Navy winged it in the ankle, causing it to skitter down the shingles and land at his feet, where he drove a lance through its heart. To the west, a line of vampires coursed down the street in a wedge, led by Braga himself as Otto and Hornsby clambered to the top of the war wagon and laid down a hail of fire that slowed but did not stop the monsters' advance.

Jed's fever burned hotter, near to searing at the edges

of the stitched flesh at his chest, while the chill settled in his belly. Braga had too many monsters with him. Just too many.

Jed whistled at Trigger Jones. "Cal, you take the right flank. Let's herd him into the cooper's."

To the outlaw's credit, he didn't ask why, just nodded and set off. The wedge crashed into the war wagon, splintering it as vampires tore in, overturning it and crushing the men defending. Jed fired the last of his holy bullets into the wedge's far side, setting two monsters smoldering and forcing them off. An arcing stream of holy water washed over the wagon from the church, forcing the vampires back. Then Cal came in from the flank, gathering up the stragglers, as if he were herding cattle. Between him and Jed, the vampires retreated into their only cover, the cooper's shop.

The cavalry man in him wanted to charge with his sword raised high, but Jed sheathed his weapon. He emptied the Peacemaker's spent cartridges and took a long second to put a fresh round in the chamber before galloping ahead. The vampires turned around as the holy water sprayed harmlessly off the cooper's exterior. Then the stream started losing power, spluttering out and dying. Jed guided Cactus towards the shop's big window. Braga stared at him from behind the glass, baleful red eyes locked on his.

"One last ride, old friend," he told Cactus and dug his fingers into the horse's neck for a good scratch. He spared a glance for his pistol, still loaded. Braga crouched in that wide stance, as if he would catch horse and rider both. Perhaps he could.

Cactus whinnied as he jumped through the glass, pushing the mob back. Jed jerked the reins aside and

Cactus wheeled away from Braga's embrace. The other vampires converged from the left and right, off the walls and from the ceiling. Jed looked past them all and lined up a shot on the tarp-covered box in the corner and fired.

Bullet met nitroglycerine.

Chapter Thirty-Eight

The cooper shop exploded in a ball of flame and roar of sundering. Splinters and dust washed over Cal, leaving him coughing and dazed, not knowing if his dizziness came from the blast, the battle, or a lingering effect of the chill in his bones. He stumbled to the remains of the war wagon and saw that the men had taken iron nails, finger-length cedar shingles, broken bones, and no few fatal bites. Two survived and Cal saw only Mayor Hornsby had a chance yet to live.

He picked Hornsby up, the man's broken body hardly a burden, and stumbled to the church. He pounded on the door, and Graham opened the bar and allowed him inside. A child gasped, but the tougher among them went to work, binding cuts and setting bones.

"Did Sheriff Scott get them?" Graham asked.

Cal could only lift a shoulder. "I don't know. I—"

Wood snapped and the remains of the cooper's shop collapsed in a great calamity of dirt, timber, and stone. From the dust and tongues of flame licking at kindling, a mutilated and stumbling Braga emerged. Gray bones poked through his form like a demonic pin cushion, though the spines were already retreating under blistered oil-slick skin as Braga stood straighter and took another step towards the church. Misshapen facial features shifted and snapped into place around red eyes glowing brighter than the growing flames rising about the wreckage. His jaw snapped into place and pushed out bone-white needle teeth, dripping with saliva.

"Hole up here and I'll deal with it," Cal told the reverend. He drew himself up and braced himself against the pew until his vision cleared. He set his hat straight and walked out with a strength he didn't feel within himself, but he'd always found a good front was the best defense in a confrontation.

Braga held a hand to his head, and pulled bits of wood from his arms, chest, and torso. His eyes drifted to Cal emerging from the church. His mouth moved. Cal shouldn't have been able to hear him from this distance, especially with the ringing in his ears from the blast, but the words appeared in his head as if Braga was standing next to him.

"Your friend couldn't face me at the end and resorted to a cowardly subterfuge, for all his bluster." Braga's eyes flicked to the faces peering out from the church windows. "The weak yearn for the strong. They secretly want someone to tell them what to do, and it is not until their wishes are answered, standing before them, that their weakness keeps them accepting what must be. Some fear change, like you, Calvin."

"No one's like me," Cal said.

"I can hear your dreaming thoughts, Calvin," Braga said. "They sing true, even if you do not. You are all alone. No wife, no family, no Wild Six, not even your duplicitous ally, Peter. You only have me, Calvin."

"I won't become you," Cal said.

Braga's laughter echoed in his head. "It's too late for that, night brother. I feel your body cooling. By next sunrise, your transformation will be complete. Come, let me hasten it along and ease your suffering."

Cal checked his right-hand Navy. Five gone, one of Graham's holy bullets left. He'd only fired once from the other Navy on his left, but it was firing plain lead. "Yeah, and then what? Just walk the earth, sucking blood and hiding in dirt holes all day?"

"You must cast your aims wider, Calvin. Right now, they go no farther than your nose, your taste no further than your next meal. When you join me, we will establish a new order in this land, seizing the legacy from those cowards on iron thrones that promise men of action all the spoils of war, while ensuring we die on their behalf. Pope or emperor, cardinal or abbot, king or president, whoever decorates himself with titles will be our enemy.

"My quarrel is not with you, but the men who used you, the men who used me. Those who send swords into battle without strength to lift one themselves, or the mettle to risk their own heart's blood watering the grass."

"So the strongest rule?" Cal asked. He touched fingertips to his pistols.

Five normal left, holy right.

"Of a sort," Braga was saying, casting away a jagged splinter and pinching the worst hole shut until it sealed. "I offer you a brotherhood, a place of belonging. I selected you for a reason, and even in your rebellion, you proved worthy where others crumbled." Braga looked back at the cooper's wreckage.

"I'm not just gonna roll over," Cal said.

"I wouldn't expect it any other way, brother." Braga set his feet, one foot forward, one foot back, with arms held in a swordsman's stance. He held no blade, but ivory-taloned fingertips meant Braga needed none.

Cal turned to face Braga square-on, set his feet wide, and welcomed the chills and fever fading from his flesh. He met Braga's eyes and only now noticed the other's oily skin was actually a moving tapestry of inky whorls sliding across each other. He wondered what other secrets a vampire's body held.

Most of all, he wondered if vampires blinked.

Chapter Thirty-Nine

BRAGA BLURRED INTO MOTION, AND CAL DREW LEFTY.

The first shot took Braga in the hip—

Braga leapt.

Cal fell aside, second bullet in the belly—

Braga's talons caught him in the thigh.

Cal hissed, sent bullets three and four, shattering bones in Braga's right arm.

Braga growled and kicked out, hitting him like a bull. Ribs cracked and crumpled.

Cal couldn't breathe, and gasped for fresh air, silently screaming through the pain while bringing the gun around and putting round five in Braga's left arm.

The vampire jerked back and left his chest open.

Cal let his left arm fall as his right hand dropped, pulled, and came up smooth with the other Navy. Graham's holy bullet falling under the hammer as the barrel swung to Braga's heart.

Braga snarled and descended. Cal's gun fired and Braga grunted, landing on top of him, but it didn't stop his jaws closing on Cal's neck, and draining the strength from his body.

"Oh, it hurts, brother," Braga said in his head, even as he was sucking his life's blood from him. "But you can save me even as you kill me. Ironic, isn't it?"

Cal couldn't form words, only feel his weakening pulse against Braga's fangs and the shadows closing in from the edges. He clutched at his chest as his heart beat its last.

Braga grew stronger, his wounds already closing.

To Cal's eyes, the world became both darker and brighter as he felt the corruption running through his body like a mountain stream. The bones in his ribs began knitting together, and a wrenching hunger pang twisted his stomach.

Braga sat back on his heels, bullet holes sealing except for the oozing hole in his chest. Braga grabbed Cal by the back of the neck and brought him close enough to catch the heady smell of his own blood dripping from his master's chin.

"Welcome to the night," Braga said.

Cal touched the calico in his pocket and didn't think. His flesh sizzled where it gripped, and the sensation redoubled when he plunged his fist through the hole in Braga's chest. Braga howled and Cal joined him as their flesh caught fire and filled the air with purple and turquoise smoke. He plunged his arm in farther until his fist found Braga's heart and he pressed Jenny's cross against it.

Braga's mouth opened in a wordless cry as his flesh withered and shrunk until he fell away from Cal's embrace, a smoldering, powdery husk that shattered on the ground. Cal opened his ruined hand, wrapping the cross's remains in its calico, then got up and stumbled down the street as dawn's light skimmed the hills.

Chapter Forty

CAL WAS NEITHER HOT NOR COLD, HE JUST WAS. HE awaited the post-battle nausea but instead found a ravenous hunger growing in his belly. He became increasingly aware of the heartbeats and delectable smells coming from the church, like steaks sizzling on the fire, though certainly not beef. He had already taken a step its way before catching himself, whereupon he turned, hitched his belt tighter, and reckoned he could stand the pangs a mite longer.

Cal found Jed's body in the flaming wreckage of the cooper shop. The man had not a mark on him, but he was certainly dead. Cal remembered coming on bodies like that in the war, just dead, perfectly intact, with charnel all around them. It wouldn't do for the man's body to burn up with the shop, so Cal dragged it clear of the flames.

The sheriff looked stern and imposing, staring up and judging Cal with unseeing eyes even as Cal arranged his limbs. Cal brushed the man's badge clean of ash and dirt before recovering his hat nearby and setting it on his chest. Cal reached to his waist and unbuckled his gun belt, exchanging the Navy .36s and baby Patterson for the manacles on Jed's rig. He gave the man a nod and headed back into the street, shielding his eyes from the dawn's glow.

Cal mounted the station steps, boots echoing on the boardwalk, passing the ticket counter, then the ticket window. "Closed," it said, and he smiled. He walked to the tracks and put his fingers to them. Not hot, not cold, just smooth metal tingling with the faintest vibrations. It was as good a place as any, he figured, so sat down on a tie and locked himself to the tracks by the wrist.

He wasn't a good man, but he tried to keep the killing to those that needed it and only take money from those that could afford it, more or less.

Calvin "Trigger" Jones always thought he'd have longer to get the scales balanced, maybe even tipped in his favor, but a sliver in him always known he'd fall short. Maybe if he'd just gone to San Francisco when the notion first took him, though the sliver told him it had likely been too late even then. He opened his right hand, the blackened skin still cracking and raw. There lay Jenny's charred cross, feeling like hot iron even through its calico wrapping, but he couldn't let it go. Really, his last chance had been back with Jenny in an Arizona town called Woodland, but Jenny was lost, and so was he.

The cross became too hot to hold, so he set it down beside him. He rubbed a corner of the calico between his fingers, brought it up to his face, and inhaled. He thought maybe he could still smell...

His eyes closed.

~

HIS EYES OPENED.

His fingers brushed cloth, then something wicked upon it seared his fingertips, a sacred icon, and he jerked back from its foul influence. Hunger ravaged him. He scented prey on the wind, close, but then panic swept through him as new senses warned of approaching danger.

The sun crept higher, nearly cresting the eastern buttes. Already, oblivion approached at a man's walking pace. The line between shadow and light was a few dozen feet away. He leapt to his feet, only to be brought up short. His arm was chained to the metal tracks. He pulled with all his strength, metal stretching but not yielding. He howled his spite into the air. He would tear the prey apart for this.

The shadows retreated, sunlight now ten feet away. He brought out his boot knife and started cutting at his wrist, only for the flesh to seal over as quickly as he could part it.

Five feet.

He pulled one last time, but couldn't help but look over his shoulder as the sun breached the ridgeline and its beams swept over him, setting him ablaze and carrying on down the tracks without a care. By the time Cal's wrist came free of the manacles, there was nothing left but ash.

Chapter Forty-One

REVEREND ONE-ARM WOULDN'T UNBOLT THE DOORS TO the church until a good half hour past sunrise. The grownups reached for Molly as she shot through the doors, but they were too tired or slow to catch her. One even made it as far as the front doors until they stopped to gape at the wreckage outside: windows shattered, doors off hinges, and the cooper's shop walls collapsed and a thick column of noxious smoke rising from within. Dead bodies shared the street with ash piles that stirred in the morning breeze. Someone behind her gasped, and another sobbed. Molly felt that she should tell them it would be alright. After all, that's what they told her at first. But she wasn't a liar, so she didn't.

Molly spotted her uncle right away, seemingly asleep with a hat on his chest in the middle of the street, but too still. He was dead too, just like mother and father. But where was the other cowboy? She walked through town and caught a shape by the tracks, an ash pile wearing the cowboy's clothes. A beaded cross lay beside the mess, weighing down a tattered bit of calico. She picked the cross up and wiped it clean with the cloth. It had been a pretty thing once and looked like it might break at any moment, but it didn't yield when Molly pressed hard with her fingers. It was stronger than it looked.

A shadow fell over her and she flinched, but it was only Reverend One-arm. He wasn't looking at her, so he couldn't see her embarrassment, and she was glad for that. He looked at the cowboy's clothes and nudged the handcuffs attached to the train tracks.

"It's Mr. Calvin," she said. "He died."

"Yes, it is, child," One-arm said. "He died." In the distance, a train whistled and both she and Reverend One-arm looked up the tracks. Molly felt the vibrations thrumming through her shoes.

"Appears the bridge is fixed," One-arm said.

"The railroad men, will they stop?" she asked.

"They have to, dear. They need our water to sustain their engines."

"Will they take us away?"

"Only if we ask them to. I expect they'll carry word on down to the next stop and help will arrive shortly thereafter."

"I don't want to stay here anymore," she said.

Reverend One-arm nodded. "I understand."

"Did Mr. Calvin's soul go to heaven to be with my mother, father, and uncle?" she asked.

Reverend One-arm didn't say anything for a spell, and Molly thought maybe he hadn't heard. But then he shook his head and said, "I don't know. It's complicated."

"It shouldn't be," Molly said.

About the Authors

Wade Peterson crafts award-winning stories that linger in your mind long after you've finished them. He's poured his heart and soul into these worlds, drawing inspiration from his love for tabletop gaming, 80s and 90s hair metal, electrical engineering mishaps, and collection of dog-eared paperback novels.

When he's not forging tales, you can find Wade unraveling the arcane mysteries of Texas barbecue in his backyard, deciphering the passive-aggressive demands of two cats, or nodding in agreement with whatever wine his wife chooses to accompany their evening feast.

David W. Wright is the co-author of edge-of-your-seat thrillers including the best-selling post-apocalyptic series *Yesterday's Gone*, the paranoid sci-fi *WhiteSpace* series, and the vigilante series, *No Justice*, as well as standalone thrillers *12*, and *Crash* which was recently optioned for a movie.

David is an accomplished, though intermittent, cartoonist who lives in [LOCATION REDACTED] with his wife and son [NAMES REDACTED.]

He is not at all paranoid.

He is "the grumpy one" on *The Story Studio Podcast* with fellow Sterling and Stone founders, Sean Platt and Johnny B. Truant.

You can email him at <u>david@sterlingandstone.net</u>
We swear, he almost never bites. Unless you feed him after midnight.

Also By David W. Wright

ForNevermore

ForNevermore Season One

ForNevermore Season Two

ForNevermore Season Three

Hidden Justice

Hidden Justice

Hidden Honor

Hidden Shame

Hidden Virtue

No Justice

No Justice

No Escape

No Hope

No Return

No Stopping

No Fear

Karma Police

Jumper

Karma Police

The Collectors

Deviant

The Fall

Homecoming

Yesterday's Gone

October's Gone

Yesterday's Gone Season One

Yesterday's Gone Season Two

Yesterday's Gone Season Three

Yesterday's Gone Season Four

Yesterday's Gone Season Five

Yesterday's Gone Season Six

Tomorrow's Gone

Tomorrow's Gone Season One

Tomorrow's Gone Season Two

Tomorrow's Gone Season Three

Available Darkness

Darkness Itself

Available Darkness Book One

Available Darkness Book Two

Available Darkness Book Three

WhiteSpace

WhiteSpace Season One

WhiteSpace Season Two

WhiteSpace Season Three

Stand Alone Novels

12

Crash

Emily's List

Threshold

Darkness Itself

The Secret Within

Sunset Blood

www.ingramcontent.com/pod-product-compliance
Lightning Source LLC
Chambersburg PA
CBHW011512100726
47899CB00010BD/3339